HELPING HIMSELF

Or

Grant Thornton's Ambition

HORATIO ALGER, JR.

Helping Himself

Horatio Alger, Jr

PO Box 2211
Fairfield, IA 52556
www.1stworldlibrary.org
First Edition

LCCN: 2004195312

Softcover ISBN: 1-4218-0143-4
Hardcover ISBN: 1-4218-0043-8
eBook ISBN: 1-4218-0243-0

Helping Himself

contributed by Tim, Ed & Rodney

in support of

1st World Library Literary Society

CHAPTER I

THE MINISTER'S SON

"I wish we were not so terribly poor, Grant," said Mrs. Thornton, in a discouraged tone.

"Is there anything new that makes you say so, mother?" answered the boy of fifteen, whom she addressed.

"Nothing new, only the same old trouble. Here is a note from Mr. Tudor, the storekeeper."

"Let me see it, mother."

Grant took a yellow envelope from his mother's hand, and drew out the inclosure, a half sheet of coarse letter paper, which contained the following lines:

"July 7, 1857.
REV. JOHN THORNTON:

DEAR SIR: Inclosed you will find a bill for groceries and other goods furnished to you in the last six months, amounting to sixty-seven dollars and thirty-four cents ($67.34). It ought to have been paid before. How you, a minister of the Gospel, can justify yourself in using goods which you don't pay for, I can't understand. If I remember rightly, the Bible says: 'Owe no man anything.' As I suppose you recognize the Bible as an authority, I expect you to pay up promptly, and oblige,

Yours respectfully, THOMAS TUDOR."

Grant looked vexed and indignant. "I think that is an impudent letter, mother," he said.

"It is right that the man should have his money, Grant."

"That is true, but he might have asked for it civilly, without taunting my poor father with his inability to pay. He would pay if he could."

"Heaven knows he would, Grant," said his mother, sighing.

"I would like to give Mr. Tudor a piece of my mind." "I would rather pay his bill. No, Grant, though he is neither kind nor considerate, we must admit that his claim is a just one. If I only knew where to turn for money!"

"Have you shown the bill to father?" asked Grant.

"No; you know how unpractical your father is. It would only annoy and make him anxious, and he would not know what to do. Your poor father has no business faculty."

"He is a very learned man," said Grant, proudly.

"Yes, he graduated very high at college, and is widely respected by his fellow ministers, but he has no aptitude for business."

"You have, mother. If you had been a man, you would have done better than he. Without your good management we should have been a good deal worse off than we are. It is the only thing that has kept our heads above water."

"I am glad you think so, Grant. I have done the best I could, but no management will pay bills without money."

It was quite true that the minister's wife was a woman of excellent practical sense, who had known how to make his small salary go very far. In this respect she differed widely from her learned husband, who in matters of business was scarcely more than a child. But, as she intimated with truth, there was something better than management, and that was ready cash.

"To support a family on six hundred dollars a year is very hard, Grant, when there are three children," resumed his mother.

"I can't understand why a man like father can't command a better salary," said Grant. "There's Rev. Mr. Stentor, in Waverley, gets fifteen hundred dollars salary, and I am sure he can't compare with father in ability."

"True, Grant, but your father is modest, and not given to blowing his own trumpet, while Mr. Stentor, from all I can hear, has a very high opinion of himself."

"He has a loud voice, and thrashes round in his pulpit, as if he were a - prophet," said Grant, not quite knowing how to finish his sentence.

"Your father never was a man to push himself forward. He is very modest."

"I suppose that is not the only bill that we owe," said Grant.

"No; our unpaid bills must amount to at least two hundred dollars more," answered his mother.

Grant whistled.

Two hundred and sixty-seven dollars seemed to him an immense sum, and so it was, to a poor minister with a family of three children and a salary of only six hundred dollars. Where to obtain so large a sum neither Grant nor his mother could possibly imagine. Even if there were anyone to borrow it from, there seemed no chance to pay back so considerable a sum.

Mother and son looked at each other in perplexity. Finally, Grant broke the silence.

"Mother," he said, "one thing seems pretty clear. I must go to work. I am fifteen, well and strong, and I ought to be earning my own living."

"But your father has set his heart upon your going to college, Grant."

"And I should like to go, too; but if I did it would be years before I could be anything but an expense and a burden, and that would make me unhappy."

"You are almost ready for college, Grant, are you not?"

"Very nearly. I could get ready for the September examination. I have only to review Homer, and brush up my Latin."

"And your uncle Godfrey is ready to help you through."

"That gives me an idea, mother. It would cost Uncle Godfrey as much as nine hundred dollars a year over and above all the help I could get from the college funds, and perhaps from teaching school this winter. Now, if he would allow me that sum for a single year and let me go to work, I could pay up all father's debts, and give him a new start. It would save Uncle Godfrey nine hundred dollars."

"He has set his heart on your going to college. I don't think he would agree to help you at all if you disappoint him."

"At any rate, I could try the experiment. Something has got to be done, mother."

"Yes, Grant, there is no doubt of that. Mr. Tudor is evidently in earnest. If we don't pay him, I think it very likely he will refuse to let us have anything more on credit. And you know there is no other grocery store in the village."

"Have you any money to pay him on account, mother?"

"I have eight dollars."

"Let me have that, and go over and see what I can do with him. We can't get along without groceries. By the way, mother, doesn't the parish owe father anything?"

"They are about sixty dollars in arrears on the salary."

"And the treasurer is Deacon Gridley?"

"Yes."

"Then I'll tell you what I will do. I'll first go over to the deacon's and try to collect something. Afterward I will call on Mr. Tudor."

"It is your father's place to do it, but he has no business faculty, and could not accomplish anything. Go, then, Grant, but remember one thing."

"What is that, mother?"

"You have a quick temper, my son. Don't allow yourself to speak hastily, or disrespectfully, even if you are disappointed. Mr. Tudor's bill is a just one, and he ought to have his money."

"I'll do the best I can, mother."

CHAPTER II

GRANT MAKES TWO BUSINESS CALLS

Deacon Gridley had a small farm, and farming was his chief occupation, but he had a few thousand dollars laid away in stocks and bonds, and, being a thrifty man, not to say mean, he managed to save up nearly all the interest, which he added to his original accumulation. He always coveted financial trusts, and so it came about that he was parish treasurer. It was often convenient for him to keep in his hands, for a month at a time, money thus collected which ought to have been paid over at once to the minister, but the deacon was a thoroughly selfish man, and cared little how pressed for money Mr. Thornton might be, as long as he himself derived some benefit from holding on to the parish funds.

The deacon was mowing the front yard of his house when Grant came up to his front gate.

"Good-morning, Deacon Gridley," said the minister's son.

"Mornin', Grant," answered the deacon. "How's your folks?"

"Pretty well in health," returned Grant, coming to

business at once, "but rather short of money."

"Ministers most gen'ally are," said Deacon Gridley, dryly.

"I should think they might be, with the small salaries they get," said Grant, indignantly.

"Some of 'em do get poorly paid," replied the deacon; "but I call six hundred dollars a pooty fair income."

"It might be for a single man; but when a minister has a wife and three children, like my father, it's pretty hard scratching."

"Some folks ain't got faculty," said the deacon, adding, complacently, "it never cost me nigh on to six hundred dollars a year to live."

The deacon had the reputation of living very penuriously, and Abram Fish, who once worked for him and boarded in the family, said he was half starved there.

"You get your milk and vegetables off the farm," said Grant, who felt the comparison was not a fair one. "That makes a great deal of difference."

"It makes some difference," the deacon admitted, "but not as much as the difference in our expenses. I didn't spend more'n a hundred dollars cash last year."

This excessive frugality may have been the reason why Mrs. Deacon Gridley was always so shabbily dressed. The poor woman had not had a new bonnet for five years, as every lady in the parish well knew.

"Ministers have some expenses that other people don't," persisted Grant.

"What kind of expenses, I'd like to know?"

"They have to buy books and magazines, and entertain missionaries, and hire teams to go on exchanges."

"That's something," admitted the deacon. "Maybe it amounts to twenty or thirty dollars a year."

"More likely a hundred," said Grant.

"That would be awful extravagant sinful waste. If I was a minister, I'd be more keerful."

"Well, Deacon Gridley, I don't want to argue with you. I came to see if you hadn't collected some money for father. Mr. Tudor has sent in his bill, and he wants to be paid."

"How much is it?"

"Sixty-seven dollars and thirty-four cents."

"You don't tell me!" said the deacon, scandalized. "You folks must be terrible extravagant."

Grant hardly knew whether to be more vexed or amused.

"If wanting to have enough to eat is extravagant," he said, "then we are."

"You must live on the fat of the land, Grant."

"We haven't any of us got the gout, nor are likely to have," answered Grant, provoked. "But let us come back to business. Have you got any money for father?"

Now it so happened that Deacon Gridley had fifty dollars collected, but he thought he knew where he could let it out for one per cent, for a month, and he did not like to lose the opportunity.

"I'm sorry to disappoint you, Grant," he answered, "but folks are slow about payin' up, and -"

"Haven't you got any money collected?" asked Grant, desperately.

"I'll tell you what I'll do," said the deacon, with a bright idea. "I've got fifty dollars of my own - say for a month, till I can make collections."

"That would be very kind," said Grant, feeling that he had done the deacon an injustice.

"Of course," the deacon resumed, hastily, "I should have to charge interest. In fact, I was goin' to lend out the money to a neighbor for a month at one per cent; but I'd just as lieve let your father have it at that price."

"Isn't that more than legal interest?" asked Grant.

"Well, you see, money is worth good interest nowadays. Ef your father don't want it, no matter. I can let the other man have it."

Grant rapidly calculated that the interest would only amount to fifty cents, and money must be had.

"I think father'll agree to your terms," he said. "I'll let you know this afternoon."

"All right, Grant. It don't make a mite of difference to me, but if your father wants the money he'll have to speak for it to-day."

"I'll see that the matter is attended to," said Grant, and he went on his way, pleased with the prospect of obtaining money for their impoverished household, even on such hard terms.

Next he made his way to Mr. Tudor's store.

It was one of those country variety stores where almost everything in the way of house supplies can be obtained, from groceries to dry goods.

Mr. Tudor was a small man, with a parchment skin and insignificant features. He was in the act of weighing out a quantity of sugar for a customer when Grant entered.

Grant waited till the shopkeeper was at leisure.

"Did you want to see me, Grant?" said Tudor.

"Yes, Mr. Tudor. You sent over a bill to our house this morning."

"And you've come to pay it. That's right. Money's tight, and I've got bills to pay in the city."

"I've got a little money for you on account," said Grant, watching Tudor's face anxiously.

"How much?" asked the storekeeper, his countenance changing.

"Eight dollars."

"Eight dollars!" ejaculated Tudor, indignantly. "Only eight dollars out of sixty-seven! That's a regular imposition, and I don't care ef your father is a minister, I stick to my words."

Grant was angry, but he remembered his mother's injunction to restrain his temper.

"We'd like to pay the whole, Mr. Tudor, if we had the money, and -"

"Do you think I can trust the whole neighborhood, and only get one dollar in ten of what's due me?" spluttered Mr. Tudor. "Ministers ought to set a better example."

"Ministers ought to get better pay," said Grant.

"There's plenty don't get as much as your father. When do you expect to pay the rest, I'd like to know? I s'pose you expect me to go on trustin', and mebbe six months from now you'll pay me another eight dollars," said the storekeeper, with withering sarcasm.

"I was going to tell you, if you hadn't interrupted me," said Grant, "that we should probably have some more money for you to-morrow."

"How much?"

"Twenty-five dollars," answered the boy, knowing that part of the money borrowed must go in other quarters.

"Will that be satisfactory?"

"That's more like!" said Tudor, calming down. "Ef you'll pay that I'll give you a leetle more time on the rest. Do you want anything this mornin'? I've got some prime butter just come in."

"I'll call for some articles this afternoon, Mr. Tudor. Here are the eight dollars. Please credit us with that sum."

"Well, I've accomplished something," said Grant to himself as he plodded homeward.

CHAPTER III

GRANT WALKS TO SOMERSET

GODFREY THORNTON, Grant's uncle, lived in the neighboring town of Somerset. He was an old bachelor, three years older than his brother, the minister, and followed the profession of a lawyer. His business was not large, but his habits were frugal, and he had managed to save up ten thousand dollars. Grant had always been a favorite with him, and having no son of his own he had formed the plan of sending him to college. He was ambitious that he should be a professional man.

It might have been supposed that he would have felt disposed to assist his brother, whose scanty salary he knew was inadequate to the needs of a family. But Godfrey Thornton was an obstinate man, and chose to give assistance in his own way, and no other. It would be a very handsome thing, he thought, to give his nephew a college education. And so, indeed, it would. But he forgot one thing. In families of limited means, when a boy reaches the age of fifteen or sixteen he is very properly expected to earn something toward the family income, and this Grant could not do while preparing for college. If his uncle could have made up his mind to give his brother a small sum annually to make up for this, all would have been well. Not that this idea had suggested itself to the Rev. John Thornton. He felt grateful for his brother's intentions toward Grant, and had bright hopes of his boy's future. But, in truth, pecuniary troubles affected him less than his wife. She was the manager, and it was for her to contrive and be anxious.

After Grant had arranged the matters referred to in the preceding chapter, he told his mother that he proposed to go to Somerset to call on his uncle.

"No, Grant, I don't object, though I should be sorry to have you lose the chance of an education."

"I have a very fair education already, mother. Of course I should like to go to college, but I can't bear to have you and father struggling with poverty. If I become a business man, I may have a better chance to help you. At any rate, I can help you sooner. If I can only induce Uncle Godfrey to give you the sum my education would cost him, I shall feel perfectly easy."

"You can make the attempt, my son, but I have doubts about your success."

Grant, however, was more hopeful. He didn't see why his uncle should object, and it would cost him no more money. It seemed to him very plain sailing, and he set out to walk to Somerset, full of courage and hope.

It was a pretty direct road, and the distance - five miles - was not formidable to a strong-limbed boy like Grant. In an hour and a half he entered the village, and soon reached the small one-story building which served his uncle as an office.

Entering, he saw his uncle busy with some papers at his desk.

The old lawyer raised his eyes as the door opened.

"So it's you, Grant, is it?" he said. "Nobody sick at home, eh?"

"No, Uncle Godfrey, we are all well."

"I was afraid some one might be sick, from your coming over. However, I suppose you have some errand in Somerset."

"My only errand is to call upon you, uncle."

"I suppose I am to consider that a compliment," said the old bachelor, not ill pleased. "Well, and when are you going to be ready for college?"

"I can be ready to enter in September," replied Grant.

"That is good. All you will have to do will be to present yourself for examination. I shall see you through, as I have promised."

"You are very kind, Uncle Godfrey," said Grant; and then he hesitated.

"It's Thornton family pride, Grant. I want my nephew to be somebody. I want you to be a professional man, and take a prominent place in the world."

"Can't I be somebody without becoming a professional man, or -"

"Or, what?" asked his uncle, abruptly.

"Getting a college education?" continued Grant.

"What does this mean?" asked the old lawyer, knitting his brow. "You're not getting off the notion of going to college, I hope?"

"I should like to go to college, uncle."

"I'm glad to hear that," said Godfrey Thornton, relieved. "I thought you might want to grow up a dunce, and become a bricklayer or something of that kind."

Somehow Grant's task began to seem more difficult than he had anticipated.

"But," continued Grant, summoning up his courage, "I am afraid it will be rather selfish."

"I can't say I understand you, Grant. As long as I am willing to pay your college bills, I don't see why there is anything selfish in your accepting my offer."

"I mean as regards father and mother."

"Don't I take you off their hands? What do you mean?"

"I mean this, Uncle Godfrey," said Grant, boldly, "I ought to be at work earning money to keep them. Father's income is very small, and -"

"You don't mean to say you want to give up going to college?" said Godfrey Thornton, hastily.

"I think I ought to, uncle."

"Why?"

"So that I can find work and help father along. You see, I should be four years in college, and three years studying a profession, and all that time my brother and sister would be growing older and more expensive, and father would be getting into debt."

Uncle Godfrey's brow wore a perceptible frown.

"Tell me who has put this idea into your head?" he said. "I am sure it isn't your father."

"No one put it into my head, Uncle Godfrey. It's my own idea."

"Humph! old heads don't grow on young shoulders, evidently. You are a foolish boy, Grant. With a liberal education you can do something for your family."

"But it is so long to wait," objected Grant.

"It will be a great disappointment to me to have you give up going to college, but of course I can't force you to go," said his uncle, coldly. "It will save me three hundred dollars a year for four years-I may say for seven, however. You will be throwing away a grand opportunity."

"Don't think I undervalue the advantage of a college training, uncle," said Grant, eagerly. "It isn't that. It's because I thought I might help father. In fact, I wanted to make a proposal to you."

"What is it?"

"You say it will cost three hundred dollars a year to keep me in college?"

"Well?"

"Would you be willing to give father two hundred a year for the next four years, and let me take care of myself in some business place?"

"So this is your proposal, is it?"

"Yes, sir."

"All I have got to say is, that you have got uncommon assurance. You propose to defeat my cherished plan, and want me to pay two hundred dollars a year in acknowledgment of your consideration."

"I am sorry you look upon it in that light, Uncle Godfrey."

"I distinctly decline your proposal. If you refuse to go to college, I wash my hands of you and your family. Do you understand that?"

"Yes, Uncle Godfrey," answered Grant, crestfallen.

"Go home and think over the matter. My offer still holds good. You can present yourself at college in September, and, if you are admitted, notify me."

The lawyer turned back to his writing, and Grant understood that the interview was over.

In sadness he started on his return walk from Somerset. He had accomplished nothing except to make his uncle angry. He could not make up his mind what to do.

He had walked about four miles when his attention was sharply drawn by a cry of terror. Looking up quickly, he saw a girl of fourteen flying along the road pursued by a drunken man armed with a big club. They were not more than thirty feet apart, and the situation was critical.

Grant was no coward, and he instantly resolved to rescue the girl if it were a possible thing.

CHAPTER IV

A TIMELY RESCUE

"I will save her if I can," said Grant to himself.

The task, however, was not an easy one. The drunken man was tall and strongly made, and his condition did not appear to interfere with his locomotion. He was evidently half crazed with drink, and his pursuit of the young girl arose probably from a blind impulse; but it was likely to be none the less serious for her. Grant saw at once that he was far from being a match for the drunkard in physical strength. If he had been timid, a regard for his personal safety would have led him to keep aloof. But he would have despised himself if he had not done what he could for the girl - stranger though she was - who was in such peril.

It chanced that Grant had cut a stout stick to help him on his way. This suggested his plan of campaign. He ran sideways toward the pursuer, and thrust his stick between his legs, tripping him up. The man fell violently forward, and lay as if stunned, breathing heavily. Grant was alarmed at first, fearing that he might be seriously hurt, but a glance assured him that his stupor was chiefly the result of his potations.

Then he hurried to overtake the girl, who, seeing what

had taken place, had paused in her flight.

"Don't be frightened," said Grant. "The man can't get up at present. I will see you home if you will tell me where you live."

"I am boarding at Mrs. Granger's, quarter of a mile back, mamma and I," answered the girl, the color, temporarily banished by fright, returning to her cheeks.

"Where did you fall in with this man?" inquired Grant.

"I was taking a walk," answered the girl, "and overtook him. I did not take much notice of him at first, and was not aware of his condition till he began to run after me. Then I was almost frightened to death, and I don't think I ever ran so fast in my life."

"You were in serious danger. He was fast overtaking you."

"I saw that he was, and I believe I should have dropped if you had not come up and saved me. How brave you were!"

Grant colored with pleasure, though he disclaimed the praise.

"Oh, it was nothing!" he said, modestly. "But we had better start at once, for he may revive."

"Oh, let us go then," exclaimed the girl in terror, and, hardly knowing what she did, she seized Grant's arm. "See, he is beginning to stir. Do come quickly!"

Clinging to Grant's arm, the two hastened away,

leaving the inebriate on the ground.

Grant now had leisure to view more closely the girl he had rescued. She was a very pretty girl, a year or two younger than himself, with a bright, vivacious manner, and her young rescuer thought her very attractive.

"Do you live round here?" she asked.

"I live in Colebrook, the village close by. I was walking from Somerset."

"I should like to know the name of the one who has done me so great a service."

"We will exchange names, if you like," said Grant, smiling. "My name is Grant Thornton. I am the son of Rev. John Thornton, who is minister in Colebrook."

"So you are a minister's son. I have always heard that minister's sons are apt to be wild," said the girl, smiling mischievously.

"I am an exception," said Grant, demurely.

"I am ready to believe it," returned his companion. "My name is Carrie Clifton; my mother is a minister's daughter, so I have a right to think well of ministers' families."

"How long have you been boarding in this neighborhood, Miss Carrie?"

"Only a week. I am afraid I shan't dare to stay here any longer."

"It is not often you would meet with such an adventure as this. I hope you won't allow it to frighten you away."

"Do you know that drunken man? Does he live nearby?"

"I think he is a stranger - a tramp. I never saw him before, and I know almost everybody who lives about here."

"I am glad he doesn't live here."

"He will probably push on his way and not come this way again during the summer."

"I hope you are right. He might try to revenge himself on you for tripping him up."

"I don't think he saw me to recognize me. He was so drunk that he didn't know what he was about. When he gets over his intoxication he probably won't remember anything that has happened."

By this time they had reached the gate of the farmhouse where Carrie was boarding, and Grant prepared to leave her.

"I think you are safe now," he said.

"Oh, but I shan't let you go yet," said the girl. "You must come in and see mother."

Grant hesitated, but he felt that he should like to meet the mother of a young lady who seemed to him so attractive, and he allowed himself to be led into the yard. Mrs. Clifton was sitting in a rustic chair under a tree behind the house. There Grant and his companion found her. Carrie poured forth her story impetuously, and then drawing Grant forward, indicated him as her rescuer.

Her mother listened with natural alarm, shuddering at the peril from which her daughter had so happily escaped.

"I cannot tell how grateful I am to you for the service you have done my daughter," she said, warmly. "You are a very brave boy. There is not one in ten who would have had the courage to act as you did."

"You praise me more than I deserve, Mrs. Clifton. I saw the man was drunk, and I did not really run much risk in what I did. I am very thankful that I was able to be of service to Miss Carrie."

"It is most fortunate that you were at hand. My daughter might have been killed."

"What do you think, mother? He is a minister's son," said Carrie, vivaciously.

"That certainly is no objection in my eyes," said Mrs. Clifton, smiling, "for I am a minister's daughter. Where does your father preach?"

"His church is only a mile distant, in the village."

"I shall hear him, then, next Sunday. Last Sunday Carrie and I were both tired, and remained at home, but I have always been accustomed to go to church somewhere."

"Papa will be here next Sunday," said Carrie. "He can only come Saturday night on account of his business."

"Does he do business in New York?" asked Grant.

"Yes; his store is on Broadway."

"We live on Madison Avenue, and whenever you are in the city we shall be very glad to have you call," said Mrs. Clifton, graciously.

"Thank you; I should like to call very much," answered Grant, who was quite sincere in what he said. "But I don't often go to New York."

"Perhaps you will get a place there some time," suggested Carrie.

"I should like to," replied Grant.

"Then your father does not propose to send you to college?" It was Mrs. Clifton who said this.

"He wishes me to go, but I think I ought to go to work to help him. He has two other children besides me."

"Is either one a girl?" asked Carrie.

"Yes; I have a sister of thirteen, named Mary."

"I wish you would bring her here to see me," said Carrie. "I haven't got acquainted with any girls yet."

Mrs. Clifton seconded the invitation, and Grant promised that he would do so. In fact, he was pleased at the opportunity it would give him of improving his acquaintance with the young lady from New York. He returned home very well pleased with his trip to Somerset, though he had failed in the object of his expedition.

CHAPTER V

MRS. THORNTON'S PEARLS

The next Sunday Mrs. Clifton and her daughter appeared at church, and Grant had the pleasure of greeting them. He was invited with his sister to take supper with them on the next Monday afternoon, and accepted the invitation. About sunset he met his new friends walking, with the addition of the husband and father, who, coming Saturday evening from New York, had felt too fatigued to attend church. Mr. Clifton, to whom he was introduced, was a portly man in middle life, who received Grant quite graciously, and made for himself acknowledgment of the service which our hero had rendered his daughter.

"If I ever have the opportunity of doing you a favor, Master Thornton, you may call upon me with confidence," he said.

Grant thanked him, and was better pleased than if he had received an immediate gift.

Meanwhile Deacon Gridley kept his promise, and advanced the minister fifty dollars, deducting a month's interest. Even with this deduction Mrs. Thornton was very glad to obtain the money. Part of it was paid on account to Mr. Tudor, and silenced his importunities for a time. As to his own plans, there was nothing for Grant to do except to continue his studies, as he might enter college after all.

If any employment should offer of a remunerative character, he felt that it would be his duty to accept it, in spite of his uncle's objections; but such chances were not very likely to happen while he remained in the country, for obvious reasons.

Three weeks passed, and again not only Mr. Tudor, but another creditor, began to be troublesome.

"How soon is your father going to pay up his bill?" asked Tudor, when Grant called at the store for a gallon of molasses.

"Very soon, I hope," faltered Grant.

"I hope so, too," answered the grocer, grimly.

"Only three weeks ago I paid you thirty-three dollars," said Grant.

"And you have been increasing the balance ever since," said Tudor, frowning.

"If father could get his salary regularly - " commenced Grant.

"That's his affair, not mine," rejoined the grocer. "I have to pay my bills regular, and I can't afford to wait months for my pay."

Grant looked uncomfortable, but did not know what to say.

"The short and the long of it is, that after this week your father must either pay up his bill, or pay cash for what articles he gets hereafter."

"Very well," said Grant, coldly. He was too proud to remonstrate. Moreover, though he felt angry, he was constrained to admit that the grocer had some reason for his course.

"Something must be done," he said to himself, but he was not wise enough to decide what that something should be.

Though he regretted to pain his mother, he felt obliged to report to her what the grocer had said.

"Don't be troubled, mother," he said, as he noticed the shade of anxiety which came over her face. "Something will turn up."

Mrs. Thornton shook her head.

"It isn't safe to trust to that, Grant," she said; "we must help ourselves."

"I wish I knew how," said Grant, perplexed.

"I am afraid I shall have to make a sacrifice," said Mrs. Thornton, not addressing Grant, but rather in soliloquy.

Grant looked at his mother in surprise. What sacrifice could she refer to? Did she mean that they must move into a smaller house, and retrench generally? That was all that occurred to him.

"We might, perhaps, move into a smaller house,

mother," said he, "but we have none too much room here, and the difference in rent wouldn't be much."

"I didn't mean that, Grant. Listen, and I will tell you what I do mean. You know that I was named after a rich lady, the friend of my mother?"

"I have heard you say so."

"When she died, she left me by will a pearl necklace and pearl bracelets, both of very considerable value."

"I have never seen you wear them, mother."

"No; I have not thought they would be suitable for the wife of a poor minister. My wearing them would excite unfavorable comment in the parish."

"I don't see whose business it would be," said Grant, indignantly.

"At any rate, just or not, I knew what would be said," Mrs. Thornton replied.

"How is it you have never shown the pearl ornaments to me, mother?"

"You were only five years old when they came to me, and I laid them away at once, and have seldom thought of them since. I have been thinking that, as they are of no use to me, I should be justified in selling them for what I can get, and appropriating the proceeds toward paying your father's debts."

"How much do you think they are worth, mother?"

"A lady to whom I showed them once said they must have cost five hundred dollars or more."

Grant whistled.

"Do you mind showing them to me, mother?" he asked.

Mrs. Thornton went upstairs, and brought down the pearl necklace and bracelets. They were very handsome and Grant gazed at them with admiration.

"I wonder what the ladies would say if you should wear them to the sewing circle," he said, humorously.

"They would think I was going over to the vanities of this world," responded his mother, smiling. "They can be of no possible use to me now, or hereafter, and I believe it will be the best thing I can do to sell them."

"Where can you sell them? No one here can afford to buy them."

"They must be sold in New York, and I must depend upon you to attend to the business for me."

"Can you trust me, mother? Wouldn't father -"

"Your father has no head for business, Grant. He is a learned man, and knows a great deal about books, but of practical matters he knows very little. You are only a boy, but you are a very sensible and trustworthy boy, and I shall have to depend upon you."

"I will do the best I can, mother. Only tell me what you want me to do."

"I wish you to take these pearls, and go to New York. You can find a purchaser there, if anywhere. I suppose it will be best to take them to some jewelry store, and drive the best bargain you can."

"When do you wish me to go, mother?"

"There can be no advantage in delay. If tomorrow is pleasant, you may as well go then."

"Shall you tell father your plan?"

"No, Grant, it might make him feel bad to think I was compelled to make a sacrifice, which, after all, is very little of a sacrifice to me. Years since I decided to trouble him as little as possible with matters of business. It could do no good, and, by making him anxious, unfitted him for his professional work."

Mrs. Thornton's course may not be considered wise by some, but she knew her husband's peculiar mental constitution, and her object at least was praiseworthy, to screen him from undue anxiety, though it involved an extra share for herself.

The next morning Grant took an early breakfast, and walked briskly toward the depot to take the first train for New York.

The fare would be a dollar and a quarter each way, for the distance was fifty miles, and this both he and his mother felt to be a large outlay. If, however, he succeeded in his errand it would be wisely spent, and this was their hope.

At the depot Grant found Tom Calder, a youth of

eighteen, who had the reputation of being wild, and had been suspected of dishonesty. He had been employed in the city, so that Grant was not surprised to meet him at the depot.

"Hello, Grant! Where are you bound?" he asked.

"I am going to New York."

"What for?"

"A little business," Grant answered, evasively. Tom was the last person he felt inclined to take into his confidence.

"Goin' to try to get a place?"

"If any good chance offers I shall accept it - that is, if father and mother are willing."

"Let's take a seat together - that's what I'm going for myself."

CHAPTER VI

GRANT GETS INTO UNEXPECTED TROUBLE

TOM CALDER was not the companion Grant would have chosen, but there seemed no good excuse for declining his company. He belonged to a rather disreputable family living in the borders of the village. If this had been all, it would not have been fair to object to him, but Tom himself bore not a very high reputation. He had been suspected more than once of stealing from his school companions, and when employed for a time by Mr. Tudor, in the village store, the latter began to miss money from the till; but Tom was so sly that he had been unable to bring the theft home to him. However, he thought it best to dispense with his services.

"What kind of a situation are you goin' to try for?" asked Tom, when they were fairly on their way.

"I don't know. They say that beggars mustn't be choosers."

"I want to get into a broker's office if I can," said Tom.

"Do you consider that a very good business?" asked Grant.

"I should say so," responded Tom, emphatically.

"Do they pay high wages?"

"Not extra, but a feller can get points, and make something out of the market."

"What's that?" asked Grant, puzzled.

"Oh, I forgot. You ain't used to the city," responded Tom, emphatically. "I mean, you find out when a stock is going up, and you buy for a rise."

"But doesn't that take considerable money?" asked Grant, wondering how Tom could raise money to buy stocks.

"Oh, you can go to the bucket shops," answered Tom.

"But what have bucket shops to do with stocks?" asked Grant, more than ever puzzled.

Tom burst into a loud laugh.

"Ain't you jolly green, though?" he ejaculated.

Grant was rather nettled at this.

"I don't see how I could be expected to understand such talk," he said, with some asperity.

"That's where it is - you can't," said Tom. "It's all like A, B, C to me, and I forgot that you didn't know anything about Wall Street. A bucket shop is where you can buy stock in small lots, putting down a dollar a share as margin. If stocks go up, you sell out on the rise, and get back your dollar minus commission,"

"Suppose they go down?"

"Then you lose what you put up."

"Isn't it rather risky?"

"Of course there's some risk, but if you have a good point there isn't much."

This was Tom Calder's view of the matter. As a matter of fact, the great majority of those who visit the bucket shops lose all they put in, and are likely sooner or later to get into difficulty; so that many employers will at once discharge a clerk or boy known to speculate in this way.

"If I had any money I'd buy some stock to-day; that is, as soon as I get to the city," continued Tom. "You couldn't lend me five dollars, could you?"

"No, I couldn't," answered Grant, shortly.

"I'd give you half the profits."

"I haven't got the money," Grant explained.

"That's a pity. The fact is, I'm rather short. However, I know plenty of fellows in the city, and I guess I can raise a tenner or so."

"Then your credit must be better in New York than in Colebrook," thought Grant, but he fore-bore to say so.

Grant was rather glad the little package of pearls was

in the pocket furthest away from Tom, for his opinion of his companion's honesty was not the highest.

When half an hour had passed, Tom vacated his seat.

"I'm going into the smoking car," he said, "to have a smoke. Won't you come with me?"

"No, thank you. I don't smoke."

"Then it's time you began. I've got a cigarette for you, if you'll try it."

"Much obliged, but I am better off without it."

"You'll soon get over that little-boy feeling. Why, boys in the city of half your age smoke."

"I am sorry to hear it."

"Well, ta-ta! I'll be back soon."

Grant was not sorry to have Tom leave him. He didn't enjoy his company, and besides he foresaw that it would be rather embarrassing if Tom should take a fancy to remain with him in the city. He didn't care to have anyone, certainly not Tom, learn on what errand he had come to the city.

Two minutes had scarcely elapsed after Tom vacated his seat, when a pleasant-looking gentleman of middle age, who had been sitting just behind them, rose and took the seat beside Grant.

"I will sit with you if you don't object," said he.

"I should be glad of your company," said Grant, politely.

"You live in the country, I infer?"

"Yes, sir."

"I overheard your conversation with the young man who has just left you. I suspect you are not very much alike."

"I hope not, sir. Perhaps Tom would say the same, for he thinks me green."

"There is such a thing as knowing too much - that isn't desirable to know. So you don't smoke?"

"No, sir."

"I wish more boys of your age could say as much. Do I understand that you are going to the city in search of employment?"

"That is not my chief errand," answered Grant, with some hesitation. "Still, if I could hear of a good chance, I might induce my parents to let me accept it."

"Where do you live, my young friend?"

"In Colebrook. My father is the minister there."

"That ought to be a recommendation, for it is to be supposed you have been carefully trained. Some of our most successful business men have been ministers' sons."

"Are you in business in New York, sir?" asked Grant, thinking he had a right by this time to ask a question.

"Yes; here is my card."

Taking the card, Grant learned that his companion was Mr. Henry Reynolds and was a broker, with an office in New Street.

"I see you are a broker, sir," said Grant. "Tom Calder wants to get a place in a broker's office."

"I should prefer that he would try some other broker," said Mr. Reynolds, smiling. "I don't want a boy who deals with the bucket shops."

At this point Tom re-entered the car, having finished his cigarette. Observing that his place had been taken, he sat down at a little distance.

"When you get ready to take a place," said the broker, "call at my office, and though I won't promise to give you a place, I shall feel well disposed to if I can make room for you."

"Thank you, sir," said Grant, gratefully. "I hope if I ever do enter your employment, I shall merit your confidence."

"I have good hopes of it. By the way, you may as well give me your name."

"I am Grant Thornton, of Colebrook," said our hero.

Mr. Reynolds entered the name in a little pocket diary, and left the seat, which Tom Calder immediately took.

"Who's that old codger?" he asked.

"The gentleman who has just left me is a New York business man."

"You got pretty thick with him, eh?"

"We talked a little."

Grant took care not to mention that Mr. Reynolds was a broker, as he knew that Tom would press for an introduction in that case.

When they reached New York, Tom showed a disposition to remain with Grant, but the latter said: "We'd better separate, and we can meet again after we have attended to our business."

A meeting place was agreed upon, and Tom went his way.

Now came the difficult part of Grant's task. Where should he go to dispose of his pearls? He walked along undecided, till he came to a large jewelry store. It struck him that this would be a good place for his purpose, and he entered.

"What can I do for you, young man?" asked a man of thirty behind the counter.

"I have some pearl ornaments I would like to sell," said Grant.

"Indeed," said the clerk, fixing a suspicious glance upon Grant; "let me see them."

Grant took out the necklace and bracelets, and passed them over. No sooner had he done so than a showily dressed lady advanced to the place where he was standing, and held out her hand for the ornaments, exclaiming: "I forbid you to buy those articles, sir. They are mine. The boy stole them from me, and I have followed him here, suspecting that he intended to dispose of them."

"That is false," exclaimed Grant, indignantly. "I never saw that woman before in my life."

"So you are a liar as well as a thief!" said the woman. "You will please give me those pearls, sir."

The clerk looked at the two contestants in indecision. He was disposed to believe the lady's statement.

CHAPTER VII

MRS. SIMPSON COMES TO GRIEF

"Surely I have a right to my own property," said the showily dressed lady in a tone of authority, which quite imposed upon the weak-minded salesman.

"I dare say you are right, ma'am," said he, hesitatingly.

"Of course I am," said she.

"If you give her those pearls, which belong to my mother, I will have you arrested," said Grant, plucking up spirit.

"Hoity-toity!" said the lady, contemptuously. "I hope you won't pay any regard to what that young thief says."

The clerk looked undecided. He beckoned an older salesman, and laid the matter before him. The latter looked searchingly at the two. Grant was flushed and excited, and the lady had a brazen front.

"Do you claim these pearls, madam?" he said.

"I do," she answered, promptly.

"How did you come by them?"

"They were a wedding present from my husband."

"May I ask your name?"

The lady hesitated a moment, then answered:

"Mrs. Simpson."

"Where do you live?"

There was another slight hesitation. Then came the answer:

"No. - Madison Avenue."

Now Madison Avenue is a fashionable street, and the name produced an impression on the first clerk.

"I think the pearls belong to the lady," he whispered.

"I have some further questions to ask," returned the elder salesman, in a low voice.

"Do you know this boy whom you charge with stealing your property?"

"Yes," answered the lady, to Grant's exceeding surprise; "he is a poor boy whom I have employed to do errands."

"Has he had the run of your house?"

"Yes, that's the way of it. He must have managed to find his way to the second floor, and opened the bureau drawer where I kept the pearls."

"What have you to say to this?" asked the elder salesman.

"Please ask the lady my name," suggested Grant.

"Don't you know your own name?" demanded the lady, sharply.

"Yes, but I don't think you do."

"Can you answer the boy's question, Mrs. Simpson?"

"Of course I can. His name is John Cavanaugh, and the very suit he has on I gave him."

Grant was thunderstruck at the lady's brazen front. She was outwardly a fine lady, but he began to suspect that she was an impostor.

"I am getting tired of this," said the so-called Mrs. Simpson, impatiently. "Will you, or will you not, restore my pearls?" "When we are satisfied that they belong to you, madam," said the elder salesman, coolly. "I don't feel like taking the responsibility, but will send for my employer, and leave the matter to him to decide."

"I hope I won't have long to wait, sir."

"I will send at once."

"It's a pretty state of things when a lady has her own property kept from her," said Mrs. Simpson, while the elder clerk was at the other end of the store, giving some instructions to a boy.

"I don't in the least doubt your claim to the articles, Mrs. Simpson," said the first salesman, obsequiously. "Come, boy, you'd better own up that you have stolen the articles, and the lady will probably let you off this time."

"Yes, I will let him off this time," chimed in the lady. "I don't want to send him to prison."

"If you can prove that I am a thief, I am willing to go," said Grant, hotly.

By this time the elder salesman had come back.

"Is your name John Cavanaugh, my boy?" he asked.

"No, sir."

"Did you ever see this lady before?"

"No, sir."

The lady threw up her hands in feigned amazement.

"I wouldn't have believed the boy would lie so!" she said.

"What is your name?"

"My name is Grant Thornton. I live in Colebrook, and my father is Rev. John Thornton."

"I know there is such a minister there. To whom do these pearls belong?"

"To my mother."

"A likely story that a country minister's wife should own such valuable pearls," said Mrs. Simpson, in a tone of sarcasm.

"How do you account for it?" asked the clerk.

"They were given my mother years since, by a rich lady who was a good friend of hers. She has never had occasion to wear them."

Mrs. Simpson smiled significantly.

"The boy has learned his story," she said. "I did not give you credit for such an imagination, John Cavanaugh."

"My name is Grant Thornton, madam," said our hero, gravely.

Five minutes later two men entered the store. One was a policeman, the other the head of the firm. When Grant's eye fell on the policeman he felt nervous, but when he glanced at the gentleman his face lighted up with pleasure.

"Why, it's Mr. Clifton," he said.

"Grant Thornton," said the jeweler, in surprise. "Why, I thought -"

"You will do me justice, Mr. Clifton," said Grant, and thereupon he related the circumstances already known to the reader.

When Mrs. Simpson found that the boy whom she had selected as an easy victim was known to the proprietor of the place, she became nervous, and only thought of escape.

"It is possible that I am mistaken," she said. "Let me look at the pearls again."

They were held up for her inspection.

"They are very like mine," she said, after a brief glance; "but I see there is a slight difference."

"How about the boy, madam?" asked the elder clerk.

"He is the very image of my errand boy; but if Mr. Clifton knows him, I must be mistaken. I am sorry to have given you so much trouble. I have an engagement to meet, and must go."

"Stop, madam!" said Mr. Clifton, sternly, interposing an obstacle to her departure, "we can't spare you yet."

"I really must go, sir. I give up all claim to the pearls."

"That is not sufficient. You have laid claim to them, knowing that they were not yours. Officer, have you ever seen this woman before?"

"Yes, sir, I know her well."

"How dare you insult me?" demanded Mrs. Simpson; but there was a tremor in her voice.

"I give her in charge for an attempted swindle," said Mr. Clifton.

"You will have to come with me, madam," said the policeman. "You may as well go quietly."

"Well, the game is up," said the woman, with a careless laugh.

"It came near succeeding, though."

"Now, my boy," said the jeweler, "I will attend to your business. You want to sell these pearls?"

"Yes, sir; they are of no use to mother, and she needs the money."

"At what do you value them?"

"I leave that to you, sir. I shall be satisfied with what you think them worth."

The jeweler examined them attentively. After his examination was concluded, he said: "I am willing to give four hundred dollars for them. Of course they cost more, but I shall have to reset them."

"That is more than I expected," said Grant, joyfully. "It will pay all our debts, and give us a little fund to help us in future."

"Do you wish the money now? There might be some risk in a boy like you carrying so much with you."

"What would you advise, Mr. Clifton?"

"That you take perhaps a hundred dollars, and let me bring the balance next Saturday night, when I come to pass Sunday at Colebrook."

"Thank you, sir; if it won't be too much trouble for you."

CHAPTER VIII

GRANT TAKES A DECISIVE STEP

Grant came home a messenger of good tidings, as his beaming face plainly showed. His mother could hardly believe in her good fortune, when Grant informed her that he had sold the pearls for four hundred dollars.

"Why, that will pay up all your father's debts," she said, "and we shall once more feel independent."

"And with a good reserve fund besides," suggested Grant.

On Saturday evening he called on Mr. Clifton, and received the balance of the purchase money. On Monday, with a little list of creditors, and his pocket full of money, he made a round of calls, and paid up everybody, including Mr. Tudor.

"I told you the bill would be paid, Mr. Tudor," he said, quietly, to the grocer.

"You mustn't feel hard on me on account of my pressing you, Grant," said the grocer, well pleased, in a conciliatory tone. "You see, I needed money to pay my bills."

"You seemed to think my father didn't mean to pay you," said Grant, who could not so easily get over what he had considered unfriendly conduct on the part of Mr. Tudor.

"No, I didn't. Of course I knew he was honest, but all the same I needed the money. I wish all my customers was as honest as your folks."

With this Grant thought it best to be contented. The time might come again when they would require the forbearance of the grocer; but he did not mean that it should be so if he could help it. For he was more than ever resolved to give up the project of going to college. The one hundred and fifty dollars which remained after paying the debts would tide them over a year, but his college course would occupy four; and then there would be three years more of study to fit him for entering a profession, and so there would be plenty of time for the old difficulties to return. If the parish would increase kis father's salary by even a hundred dollars, they might get along; but there was such a self-complacent feeling in the village that Mr. Thornton was liberally paid, that he well knew there was no chance of that.

Upon this subject he had more than one earnest conversation with his mother.

"I should be sorry to have you leave home," she said; "but I acknowledge the force of your reasons."

"I shouldn't be happy at college, mother," responded Grant, "if I thought you were pinched at home."

"If you were our only child, Grant, it would

be different."

"That is true; but there are Frank and Mary who would suffer. If I go to work I shall soon be able to help you take care of them."

"You are a good and unselfish boy, Grant," said his mother.

"I don't know about that, mother; I am consulting my own happiness as well as yours."

"Yet you would like to go to college?"

"If we had plenty of money, not otherwise. I don't want to enjoy advantages at the expense of you all."

"Your Uncle Godfrey will be very angry," said Mrs. Thornton, thoughtfully.

"I suppose he will, and I shall be sorry for it. I am grateful to him for his good intentions toward me, and I have no right to expect that he will feel as I do about the matter. If he is angry, I shall be sorry, but I don't think it ought to influence me."

"You must do as you decide to be best, Grant. It is you who are most interested. But suppose you make up your mind to enter upon a business career, what chance have you of obtaining a place?"

"I shall call upon Mr. Reynolds, and see if he has any place for me."

"Who is Mr. Reynolds?" asked his mother, in some surprise.

"I forgot that I didn't tell you of the gentleman whose acquaintance I made on my way up to the city. He is a Wall Street broker. His attention was drawn to me by something that he heard, and he offered to help me, if he could, to get employment."

"It would cost something to go to New York, and after all there is no certainty that he could help you," said Mrs. Thornton, cautiously.

"That is true, mother, but I think he would do something for me."

However Grant received a summons to New York on other business. Mrs. Simpson, as she called herself, though she had no right to the name, was brought up for trial, and Grant was needed as a witness. Of course his expenses were to be paid. He resolved to take this opportunity to call at the office of Mr. Reynolds.

I do not propose to speak of Mrs. Simpson's trial. I will merely say that she was found guilty of the charge upon which she had been indicted, and was sentenced to a term of imprisonment.

When Grant was released from his duties as witness, he made his way to Wall Street, or rather New Street, which branches out from the great financial thoroughfare, and had no difficulty in finding the office of Mr. Reynolds.

"Can I see Mr. Reynolds?" he asked of a young man, who was writing at a desk.

"Have you come to deliver stock? If so, I will take charge of it."

"No," answered Grant; "I wish to see him personally."

"He is at the Stock Exchange just at present. If you will take a seat, he will be back in twenty minutes, probably."

Grant sat down, and in less than the time mentioned, Mr. Reynolds entered the office. The broker, who had a good memory for faces, at once recognized our hero.

"Ha, my young friend from the country," he said; "would you like to see me?"

"When you are at leisure, sir," answered Grant, well pleased at the prompt recognition.

"You will not have to wait long. Amuse yourself as well as you can for a few minutes."

Promptness was the rule in Mr. Reynolds' office. Another characteristic of the broker was, that he was just as polite to a boy as to his best customer. This is, I am quite aware, an unusual trait, and, therefore, the more to be appreciated when we meet with it.

Presently Mr. Reynolds appeared at the door of his inner office, and beckoned to Grant to enter.

"Take a seat, my young friend," he said; "and now let me know what I can do for you."

"When I met you in the cars," said Grant, "you invited me, if I ever wanted a position, to call upon you, and you would see if you could help me."

"Very true, I did. Have you made up your mind to seek

a place?"

"Yes, sir."

"Are your parents willing you should come to New York?"

"Yes, sir. That is, my mother is willing, and my father will agree to whatever she decides to be best."

"So far so good. I wouldn't engage any boy who came against his parents' wishes. Now let me tell you that you have come at a very favorable time. I have had in my employ for two years the son of an old friend, who has suited me in every respect; but now he is to go abroad with his father for a year, and I must supply his place. You shall have the place if you want it."

"Nothing would suit me better," said Grant, joyfully. "Do you think I would be competent to fulfill the duties?"

"Harry Becker does not leave me for two weeks. He will initiate you into your duties, and if you are as quick as I think you are at learning, that will be sufficient."

"When shall I come, sir?"

"Next Monday morning. It is now Thursday, and that will give you time to remove to the city."

"Perhaps I had better come Saturday, so as to get settled in a boarding-house before going to work. Could you recommend some moderate priced boarding-house, Mr. Reynolds?"

"For the first week you may come to my house as my guest. That will give you a chance to look about you. I live at 58 West 3-th Street. You had better take it down on paper. You can come any time on Monday. That will give you a chance to spend Sunday at home, and you need not go to work till Tuesday."

Grant expressed his gratitude in suitable terms, and left the office elated at his good fortune. A surprise awaited him. At the junction of Wall and New Streets he came suddenly upon a large-sized bootblack, whose face looked familiar.

"Tom Calder!" he exclaimed. "Is that you?"

CHAPTER IX

'UNCLE GODFREY PARTS FROM GRANT

When Tom Calder turned round and saw who had addressed him, he turned red with mortification, and he tried to hide his blacking box. He was terribly mortified to have it known that he had been forced into such a business. If Tom had nothing worse to be ashamed of he need not have blushed, but he was suffering from false shame.

"When did you come to the city?" he stammered.

"Only this morning."

"I suppose you are surprised to see me in this business," said Tom, awkwardly.

"There is nothing to be ashamed of," said Grant. "It is an honest business."

"It's an awful come down for me," said Tom, uncomfortably. "The fact is, I've had hard luck."

"I am sorry to hear that," said Grant.

"I expected a place in Wall Street, but I came just too late, and things are awful dull anyway. Then I was robbed of my money."

"How much?" asked Grant, curiously, for he didn't believe a word of it.

"Eight dollars and thirty-three cents," replied Tom, glibly.

"I thought you were too smart to be robbed," said Grant, slyly. "If it had been a green boy from the country like me, now, it wouldn't have been surprising."

"I was asleep when I was robbed," explained Tom, hurriedly. "A fellow got into my room in the night, and picked my pocket. I couldn't help that, now, could I?"

"I suppose not."

"So I had to get something to do, or go back to Colebrook. I say, Grant -"

"Well?"

"Don't you tell any of the fellers at home what business I'm in, that's a good fellow."

"I won't if you don't want me to," said Grant.

"You see, it's only a few days till I can get something else to do."

"It's a great deal better blacking boots than being idle, in my opinion," said Grant.

"That's the way I look at it. But you didn't tell me what

you came to the city for?"

"I'm coming here for good," announced Grant.

"You haven't got a place, have you?" ejaculated Tom, in surprise.

"Yes, I am to enter the office of Mr. Reynolds, a stock broker. There is his sign."

"You don't say so I. Why, that's just the sort of place I wanted. How did you get the chance?"

"I got acquainted with Mr. Reynolds on board the cars that day we came to New York together."

"And you asked him for the place?"

"I asked him this morning."

"You might have given me the chance," grumbled Tom, enviously. "You knew it was the sort of place I was after."

"I don't think I was called upon to do that," said Grant, smiling. "Besides, he wouldn't have accepted you."

"Why not? Ain't I as smart as you, I'd like to know?" retorted Tom Calder, angrily.

"He heard us talking in the cars, and didn't like what you said."

"What did I say?"

"He doesn't approve of boys smoking cigarettes and

going to bucket shops. You spoke of both."

"How did he hear?"

"He was sitting just behind us."

"Was it that old chap that was sittin' with you when I came back from the smoking car?"

"Yes."

"Just my luck," said Tom, ruefully.

"When are you goin' to work?" asked Tom, after a pause.

"Next Monday."

"Where are you going to board? We might take a room together, you know. It would be kind of social, as we both come from the same place."

It did not occur to Grant that the arrangement would suit him at all, but he did not think it necessary to say so. He only said: "I am going to Mr. Reynolds' house, just at first."

"You don't say so! Why, he's taken a regular fancy to you."

"If he has, I hope he won't get over it."

"I suppose he lives in a handsome brownstone house uptown."

"Very likely; I've never seen the house."

"Well, some folks has luck, but I ain't one of 'em," grumbled Tom.

"Your luck is coming, I hope, Tom."

"I wish it would come pretty soon, then; I say, suppose your folks won't let you take the place?" he asked, suddenly, brightening up.

"They won't oppose it." "I thought they wanted you to go to college."

"I can't afford it. It would take too long before I could earn anything, and I ought to be helping the family."

"I'm goin' to look out for number one," said Tom, shrugging his shoulders. "That's all I can do."

Tom's mother was a hard-working woman, and had taken in washing for years. But for her the family would often have lacked for food. His father was a lazy, intemperate man, who had no pride of manhood, and cared only for himself. In this respect Tom was like him, though the son had not as yet become intemperate.

"I don't think there is any chance of my giving up the place," answered Grant. "If I do, I will mention your name."

"That's a good fellow."

Grant did not volunteer to recommend Tom, for he could not have done so with a clear conscience. This omission, however, Tom did not notice.

"Well, Tom, I must be going. Good-by, and good luck."

Grant went home with a cheerful face, and announced his good luck to his mother.

"I am glad you are going to your employer's house," she said. "I wish you could remain there permanently."

"So do I, mother; but I hope at any rate to get a comfortable boarding place. Tom Calder wants to room with me."

"I hope you won't think of it," said Mrs. Thornton, alarmed.

"Not for a moment. I wish Tom well, but I shouldn't like to be too intimate with him. And now, mother, I think I ought to write to Uncle Godfrey, and tell him what I have decided upon."

"That will be proper, Grant." Grant wrote the following letter, and mailed it at once:

"DEAR UNCLE GODFREY:

I am afraid you won't like what I have to tell you, but I think it is my duty to the family to give up the college course you so kindly offered me, in view of father's small salary and narrow means. I have been offered a place in the office of a stock broker in New York, and have accepted it. I enter upon my duties next Monday morning. I hope to come near paying my own way, and before very long to help father. I know you will be disappointed, Uncle Godfrey, and I hope you won't think I don't appreciate your kind offer, but I think it would be selfish in me to accept it. Please do forgive me, and believe me to be

Your affectionate nephew, GRANT THORNTON."

In twenty-four hours an answer came to this letter. It ran thus:

"NEPHEW GRANT:

I would not have believed you would act so foolishly and ungratefully. It is not often that such an offer as mine is made to a boy. I did think you were sensible enough to understand the advantages of a professional education. I hoped you would do credit to the name of Thornton, and keep up the family reputation as a man of learning and a gentleman. But you have a foolish fancy for going into a broker's office, and I suppose you must be gratified. But you needn't think I will renew my offer. I wash my hands of you from this time forth, and leave you to your own foolish course. The time will come when you will see your folly.

GODFREY THORNTON."

Grant sighed as he finished reading this missive. He felt that his uncle had done him injustice. It was no foolish fancy, but a conscientious sense of duty, which had led him to sacrifice his educational prospects.

On Monday morning he took the earliest train for New York.

CHAPTER X

A DAY IN WALL STREET

Grant went at once on his arrival in the city to Mr. Reynolds' office. He had in his hand a well-worn valise containing his small stock of clothing. The broker was just leaving the office for the Stock Exchange as Grant entered.

"So you are punctual," he said, smiling.

"Yes, sir, I always on time."

"That is an excellent habit. Here, Harry."

In answer to this summons, Harry Becker, a boy two years older and correspondingly larger than Grant, came forward. He was a pleasant-looking boy, and surveyed Grant with a friendly glance.

"Harry," said Mr. Reynolds, "this is your successor. Do me the favor of initiating him into his duties, so that when you leave me he will be qualified to take your place."

"All right, sir."

The broker hurried over to the Exchange, and the two

boys were left together.

"What is your name?" asked the city boy.

"Grant Thornton."

"Mine is Harry Becker. Are you accustomed to the city?"

"No, I am afraid you will find me very green," answered Grant.

"You are not the boy to remain so long," said Harry, scrutinizing him attentively.

"I hope not. You are going to Europe, Mr. Reynolds tells me."

"Yes, the governor is going to take me."

"The governor?"

"My father, I mean," said Harry, smiling.

"I suppose you are not sorry to go?"

"Oh, no; I expect to have a tip-top time. How would you like it?"

"Very much, if I could afford it, but at present I would rather fill your place in the office. I am the son of a poor country minister, and must earn my own living."

"How did you get in with Mr. Reynolds?" asked Harry.

Grant told him. "Is he easy to get along with?" he

inquired, a little anxiously.

"He is very kind and considerate. Still he is stanch, and expects a boy to serve him faithfully."

"He has a right to expect that."

"As I am to break you in, you had better go about with me everywhere. First, we will go to the post-office."

The two boys walked to Nassau Street, where the New York post-office was then located. Harry pointed out the box belonging to the firm, and producing a key opened it, and took out half a dozen letters.

"There may be some stock orders in these letters," he said; "we will go back to the office, give them to Mr. Clark to open, and then you can go with me to the Stock Exchange."

Ten minutes later they entered the large room used by the brokers as an Exchange. Grant looked about him in undisguised astonishment. It seemed like a pandemonium. The room was full of men, shouting, gesticulating and acting like crazy men. The floor was littered with fragments of paper, and on a raised dais were the officers of the Exchange, the chief among them, the chairman, calling rapidly the names of a long list of stocks. Each name was followed by a confused shouting, which Grant learned afterward to be bids for the stock named. There were several groups of brokers, each apparently interested in some leading security. In each of the galleries, one at each end, overlooking the stock room, curious spectators were watching what was going on.

Harry Decker was amused at Grant's look of surprise and bewilderment.

"You'll get used to it in time," he said. "Say - there is Mr. Reynolds. I must speak to him."

Mr. Reynolds stood near a placard on which, in prominent letters, was inscribed "Erie." Harry handed him a paper, which he took, glanced at quickly, and then resumed his bidding.

"He has just bought one thousand Erie," said Harry, aside, to Grant.

"One thousand?"

"Yes, a thousand shares, at fifty-five."

"Fifty-five dollars?"

"Yes."

"Why, that will make fifty-five thousand dollars," ejaculated Grant, in wonder.

"Yes, that is one of the orders I brought over just now."

"A man must have a great deal of capital to carry on this business, if that is only an item of a single day's business."

"Yes, but not so much as you may imagine. I can't explain now, but you'll understand better as you go on. Now we'll go back and see if there's anything to do in the office."

Not long afterward Harry had to come back to the Exchange again, and Grant came with him. He found something new to surprise him.

A tall man of dignified presence was walking across the floor, when a fellow member with a sly stroke sent his tall hat spinning across the floor. When the victim turned the mischief-maker was intent upon his memorandum book, and the tall man's suspicions fell upon a short, stout young man beside him. With a vigorous sweep he knocked the young man's hat off, saying, "It's a poor rule that don't work both ways."

This led to a little scrimmage, in which a dozen were involved. The brokers, staid, middle-aged men, most of them, seemed like a pack of school boys at recess. Grant surveyed the scene with undisguised astonishment.

"What does it mean, Harry?" he asked.

"Oh, that's a very common occurrence," said Harry, smiling.

"I never saw grown men acting so. Won't there be a fight?"

"Oh, it's all fun. The brokers are unlike any other class of men in business hours," explained Harry. "It's one of the customs of the place."

Just then, to his astonishment, Grant saw his employer, Mr. Reynolds, pursuing his hat, which was rolling over the floor. He was about to run to his assistance, but Harry stopped him.

"No interference is allowed," he said. "Leave them to their fun. I used to think it strange myself, when I first came into the Exchange, but I'm used to it now. Now we may as well go back to the office."

There is no occasion to follow the boys through the day's routine. Grant found his companion very obliging, and very ready to give him the information he needed. Many boys would have been supercilious and perhaps been disposed to play tricks on a country boy, but Harry was not one of them. He took a friendly interest in Grant, answered all his questions, and did his best to qualify him for the position he was to assume.

Before the office closed, Grant and his new friend went to the bank to make a deposit of money and checks. The deposit amounted to about twenty thousand dollars.

"There must be plenty of money in New York," said Grant. "Why, up in Colebrook, if a man were worth twenty thousand dollars he would be considered a rich man."

"It takes a good deal more than that to make a man rich in New York. In the stock business a man is likely to do a larger business in proportion to his capital than in the mercantile business."

On their way back from the bank, Grant came face to face with Tom Calder. Tom was busily engaged in talking to a companion, some years older than himself, and didn't observe Grant. Grant was by no means prepossessed in favor of this young man, whose red and mottled face, and bold glance made him look far from respectable.

"Do you know those fellows?" asked Harry Becker.

"The youngest one is from Colebrook."

"He is in bad company. I hope he is not an intimate friend of yours?"

"Far from it. Still, I know him, and am sorry to see him with such a companion."

At four o'clock Mr. Reynolds proposed to go home. He beckoned to Grant to accompany him.

CHAPTER XI

GRANT MAKES A FRIEND

"What do you think of your first day in Wall Street?" asked Mr. Reynolds, kindly.

"I have found it very interesting," answered Grant.

"Do you think you shall like the business?"

"Yes, sir, I think so."

"Better than if you had been able to carry out your original plan, and go to college?"

"Yes, sir, under the circumstances, for I have a better prospect of helping the family."

"That feeling does you credit. Have you any brothers and sisters?"

"One of each, sir."

"I have but one boy, now nine years old. I am sorry to say he is not strong in body, though very bright and quick, mentally. I wish he were more fond of play and would spend less time in reading and study."

"I don't think that is a common complaint among boys, sir."

"No, I judge not from my own remembrance and observation. My wife is dead, and I am such a busy man that I am not able to give my boy as much attention as I wish I could. My boy's health is the more important to me because I have no other child."

Grant's interest was excited, and he looked forward to meeting his employer's son, not without eagerness. He had not long to wait.

The little fellow was in the street in front of the house when his father reached home. He was a slender, old-fashioned boy in appearance, who looked as if he had been in the habit of keeping company with grown people. His frame was small, but his head was large. He was pale, and would have been plain, but for a pair of large, dark eyes, lighting up his face.

"Welcome home, papa," he said, running up to meet Mr. Reynolds.

The broker stooped over and kissed his son. Then he said: "I have brought you some company, Herbert. This is Grant Thornton, the boy I spoke to you about."

"I am glad to make your acquaintance," said the boy, with old-fashioned courtesy, offering his hand.

"And I am glad to meet you, Herbert," responded Grant, pleasantly.

The little boy looked up earnestly in the face of his father's office boy.

"I think I shall like you," he said.

Mr. Reynolds looked pleased, and so did Grant.

"I am sure we shall be very good friends," said our hero.

"Herbert," said his father, "will you show Grant the room he is to occupy?"

"It is next to mine, isn't it, papa?"

"Yes, my son."

"Come with me," said Herbert, putting his hand in Grant's. "I will show you the way."

Grant, who was only accustomed to the plain homes in his native village, was impressed by the evidence of wealth and luxury observable in the house of the stock broker. The room assigned to him was small, but it was very handsomely furnished, and he almost felt out of place in it. But it was not many days, to anticipate matters a little, before he felt at home.

Herbert took Grant afterward into his own room.

"See my books," he said, leading the way to a book-case, containing perhaps a hundred volumes, the majority of a juvenile character, but some suited to more mature tastes. "Do you like reading?" asked Grant.

"I have read all the books you see here," answered Herbert, "and some of papa's besides. I like to read better than to play."

"But you ought to spend some of your time in play, or you will not grow up healthy."

"That is what papa says. I try to play some, but I don't care much about it."

Grant was no longer surprised at the little boy's delicacy. It was clear that he needed more amusement and more exercise. "Perhaps," he thought, "I can induce Herbert to exercise more."

"When do you take dinner?" he asked.

"At half-past six. There is plenty of time."

"Then suppose we take a little walk together. We shall both have a better appetite."

"I should like to," replied Herbert; "that is, with you. I don't like to walk alone."

"How far is Central Park from here?"

"A little over a mile."

"I have never seen it. Would you mind walking as far as that?"

"Oh, no."

So the two boys walked out together. They were soon engaged in an animated conversation, consisting, for the most part, of questions proposed by Grant, and answers given by Herbert.

Not far from the park they came to a vacant lot where

some boys were playing ball.

"Now, if we only had a ball, Herbert," said Grant, "we might have a little amusement."

"I've got a ball in my pocket, but I don't use it much."

"Let me see it."

Herbert produced the ball, which proved to be an expensive one, better than any Grant had ever owned.

"There, Herbert, stand here, and I will place myself about fifty feet away. Now, throw it to me, no matter how swiftly."

They were soon engaged in throwing the ball to each other. Grant was a good ball player, and he soon interested the little boy in the sport. Our hero was pleased to see Herbert's quiet, listless manner exchanged for the animation which seemed better suited to a boy.

"You are improving, Herbert," he said, after a while. "You would make a good player in time."

"I never liked it before," said the little boy. "I never knew there was so much fun in playing ball."

"We shall have to try it every day. I suppose it is about time to go home to supper."

"And we haven't been to Central Park, after all."

"That will do for another day. Are boys allowed to play ball in the park?"

"Two afternoons in the week, I believe, but I never played there."

"We shall have to try it some day."

"I should like to play - with you."

They reached home in full time for dinner. At the dinner table Mr. Reynolds was struck by the unusually bright and animated face of his son, and his good appetite.

"What have you been doing to make you so hungry, Herbert?" he asked.

"I took a walk with Grant, and we had a fine game of ball."

"I am glad to hear it," said the broker, much pleased. "If you want to become stout and strong like Grant, that is the best thing for you to do."

"I never liked playing ball before, papa."

"That is a compliment to you, Grant," said the broker, smiling.

"I think," he said to the prim, elderly lady who presided over the household, acting as housekeeper, "Herbert will be the better for having a boy in the house."

"I don't know about that," said Mrs. Estabrook, stiffly. "When he came into the house he had mud on his clothes. He never did that till this boy came."

"I won't complain of that, if his health is improved."

Mrs. Estabrook, who was a poor relation of Herbert's mother, pursed up her mouth, but did not reply. In her eyes, it was more important that a boy should keep his clothes whole and clean than to have color in his cheeks, and health in his frame.

"I hope that boy won't stay here long," she thought, referring, of course, to Grant. "He'll quite spoil Herbert by making him rough and careless of his appearance."

"Well, Herbert, and how do you like Grant?" asked Mr. Reynolds, as his son was bidding him good-night before going to bed.

"I am so glad you brought him here, papa. I shall have good times now. You'll let him stay all the time, won't you?"

"I'll see about it, Herbert," answered his father, smiling.

CHAPTER XII

MRS. ESTABROOK'S PLANS

Grant was going home with Mr. Reynolds at the close of the fourth day, when it occurred to him to say what had been in his mind for some time: "Isn't it time, Mr. Reynolds, for me to be looking out for a boarding place?"

The broker smiled, and said with assumed concern: "Are you dissatisfied with your present boarding place?"

"How could I be, sir?" returned Grant, earnestly. "But you told me I could stay with you a week, while I was looking about for a suitable place to board."

"That is true. Now, however, there is a difficulty about your making a change."

"What is that, sir?"

"Herbert would not give his consent. The fact is, Grant, Herbert finds so much pleasure in your society, and derives so much advantage from the increased exercise you lead him to take, that I think you will have to make up your mind to stay."

Grant's face showed the pleasure he felt.

"I shall be very glad to stay, Mr. Reynolds," he answered, "if you are willing to have me."

"I had this in view from the first," said the broker, "but I wanted to see how you and Herbert got along. I wished to be sure, also, that your influence on him would be good. Of that I can have no doubt, and I am glad to receive you as a member of my family."

There was one member of the household, however, who was not so well pleased with the proposed arrangement. This was Mrs. Estabrook, the housekeeper.

As the week drew to a close, she said, one evening after the boys had retired:

"How much longer is the office boy to stay here, Mr. Reynolds?"

"Why do you ask?" inquired the broker.

"Only with reference to domestic arrangements," answered the housekeeper, disconcerted.

"He will remain for a considerable time, Mrs. Estabrook."

"I - I thought he was only going to stay a week."

"He is company for Herbert, and I think it desirable to keep him."

"Herbert soils his clothes a deal more now than he used to do," said the housekeeper, discontentedly. "I am sure I don't know where the other boy carries him."

"Nor I, but I am not afraid to trust him with Grant. As to the clothes, I consider them of very small account, compared with my boy's health."

Mrs. Estabrook knitted in silence for five minutes. She was by no means pleased with her employer's plan, having taken a dislike to Grant, for which, indeed, her chief reason was jealousy. She had a stepson, a young man of twenty-one, in Mr. Reynolds' office, whom she would like to have in the house in place of Grant. But Mr. Reynolds had never taken notice of her occasional hints to that effect. The housekeeper's plans were far-reaching. She knew that Herbert was delicate, and doubted if he would live to grow up. In that case, supposing her stepson had managed to ingratiate himself with the broker, why might he not hope to become his heir? Now this interloper, as she called Grant, had stepped into the place which her own favorite - his name was Willis Ford - should have had. Mrs. Estabrook felt aggrieved, and unjustly treated, and naturally incensed at Grant, who was the unconscious cause of her disappointment. She returned to the charge, though, had she been wiser, she would have foreborne.

"Do you think a poor boy like this Grant Thornton is a suitable companion for a rich man's son, Mr. Reynolds? Excuse me for suggesting it, but I am so interested in dear Herbert."

"Grant Thornton is the son of a country minister, and has had an excellent training," said the broker, coldly. "The fact that he is poor is no objection in my eyes. I think, Mrs. Estabrook, we will dismiss the subject. I think myself competent to choose my son's associates."

"I hope you will excuse me," said the housekeeper, seeing that she had gone too far. "I am so attached to the dear child."

"If you are, you will not object to the extra trouble you may have with his clothes, since his health is benefited."

"That artful young beggar has wound his way into his employer's confidence," thought Mrs. Estabrook, resentfully, "but it may not be always so."

A few minutes later, when the housekeeper was in her own sitting-room, she was told that Willis Ford wanted to see her.

Mrs. Estabrook's thin face lighted up with pleasure, for she was devotedly attached to her stepson.

"Bring him up here at once," she said.

A minute later the young man entered the room. He was a thin, sallow-complexioned young man, with restless, black eyes, and a discontented expression - as of one who thinks he is not well used by the world.

"Welcome, my dear boy," said the housekeeper, warmly. "I am so glad to see you."

Willis submitted reluctantly to his stepmother's caress, and threw himself into a rocking chair opposite her.

"Are you well, Willis?" asked Mrs. Estabrook, anxiously.

"Yes, I'm well enough," muttered the young man.

"I thought you looked out of sorts."

"I feel so."

"Is anything the matter?"

"Yes; I'm sick of working at such starvation wages."

"I thought fifteen dollars a week a very good salary. Only last January you were raised three dollars."

"And I expected to be raised three dollars more on the first of July."

"Did you apply to Mr. Reynolds?"

"Yes, and he told me I must wait till next January."

"I think he might have raised you, if only on account of the connection between our families."

"Perhaps he would if you would ask him, mother."

"I will when there is a good opportunity. Still, Willis, I think fifteen dollars a week very comfortable."

"You don't know a young man's expenses, mother."

"How much do you pay for board, Willis?"

"Six dollars a week. I have a room with a friend, or I should have to pay eight."

"That leaves you nine dollars a week for all other

expenses. I think you might save something out of that."

"I can't. I have clothes to buy, and sometimes I want to go to the theatre, and in fact, nine dollars don't go as far as you think. Of course, a woman doesn't need to spend much. It's different with a young man."

"Your income would be a good deal increased if you had no board to pay."

"Of course. You don't know any generous minded person who will board me for nothing, do you?"

"There's a new office boy in your office, isn't there?"

"Yes, a country boy."

"Did you know he was boarding here?"

"No; is he?"

"Mr. Reynolds told me to-night he was going to keep him here permanently, as a companion for his little son."

"Lucky for him."

"I wish Mr. Reynolds would give you a home here."

"I would rather he would make it up in money, and let me board where I please."

"But you forget. It would give you a chance to get him interested in you, and if Herbert should die, you might take his place as heir."

"That would be a splendid idea, but there's no prospect of it. It isn't for me."

"It may be for the office boy. He's an artful boy, and that's what he's working for, in my opinion."

"I didn't think the little beggar was so evil-headed. He seems quiet enough."

"Still waters run deep. You'd better keep an eye on him, and I'll do the same."

"I will."

The next day Grant was puzzled to understand why Willis Ford spoke so sharply to him, and regarded him with such evident unfriendliness.

"What have I done to offend you?" he thought.

CHAPTER XIII

TWO VIEWS OF TOM CALDER

Thus far nothing had been said about the compensation Grant was to receive for his work in the broker's office. He did not like to ask, especially as he knew that at the end of the first week the matter would be settled. When he found that he was to remain for the present at the house of his employer he concluded that his cash pay would be very small, perhaps a dollar a week. However, that would be doing quite as well as if he paid his own board elsewhere, while he enjoyed a much more agreeable and luxurious home. He would be unable to assist his father for a year or two; but that was only what he had a right to expect.

When Saturday afternoon came, Mr. Reynolds said: "By the way, Grant, I must pay you your week's wages. I believe no sum was agreed upon."

"No, sir."

"We will call it six dollars. Will that be satisfactory?"

"Very much so, Mr. Reynolds; but there will be a deduction for board."

Mr. Reynolds smiled.

"That is a different matter," he said. "That comes to you as Herbert's companion. It is worth that to me to have my boy's happiness increased."

Grant was overjoyed at the bright prospect opened before him, and he said, with glowing face: "You are very kind, Mr. Reynolds. Now I shall be able to help my father."

"That is very creditable to you, my boy. Willis, you may pay Grant six dollars."

Willis Ford did so, but he looked very glum. He estimated that, including his board, Grant would be in receipt of twelve dollars a week, or its equivalent, and this was only three dollars less than he himself received, who had been in the office five years and was a connection of the broker.

"It's a shame," he thought, "that this green, country boy should be paid nearly as much as I - I must call and tell mother."

Grant was a very happy boy that evening. He resolved to lay aside three dollars a week to send to his mother, to save up a dollar a week and deposit it in some savings bank, and make the other two dollars answer for his clothing and miscellaneous expenses.

On the next Monday afternoon Grant walked home alone, Mr. Reynolds having some business which delayed him. He thought he would walk up Broadway, as there was much in that crowded thoroughfare to amuse and interest him.

Just at the corner of Canal Street he came across Tom

Calder. Tom was standing in a listless attitude with his hands in his pockets, with apparently no business cares weighing upon his mind.

"Hello, Grant!" he said, with sudden recognition.

"How are you, Tom?"

"I'm all right, but I'm rather hard up."

Grant was not surprised to hear that.

"You see, there's a feller owes me seven dollars, and I can't get it till next week," continued Tom, watching Grant's face to see if hebelieved it.

Grant did not believe it, but did not think it necessary to say so.

"That's inconvenient," he remarked.

"I should say it was. You couldn't lend me a couple of dollars, could you?"

"I don't think I could."

Tom looked disappointed.

"How much do you get?" he asked.

"Six dollars a week."

"That's pretty good, for a boy like you. I wish you'd take a room with me. It would come cheaper."

"I shall stay where I am for the present," said Grant.

He did not care to mention, unless he were asked, that he was making his home at the house of Mr. Reynolds, as it might either lead to a call from Tom, whom he did not particularly care to introduce to his new friends, or might lead to a more pressing request for a loan.

"Where are you boarding?" asked Grant, after a pause.

"In Clinton Place. I have a room there, and get my meals where I like. There's a chap from your office that lives in the same house."

"Who is it?" asked Grant, anxiously.

"It's Willis Ford."

"Is that so?" returned Grant, in surprise. "Do you know him?"

"Only a little. I don't like him. He's too stuck up."

Grant made no comment, but in his heart he agreed with Tom.

"Are you doing anything?" he asked.

"Not just yet," answered Tom, "I expect a good job soon. You haven't a quarter to spare, have you?" Grant produced the desired sum and handed it to his companion. He didn't fancy Tom, but he was willing to help him in a small way.

"Thanks," said Tom. "That'll buy my supper. I'll give it back to you in a day or two."

Grant did not think there was much likelihood of that,

but felt that he could afford to lose this small sum.

Four days later he met Tom in Wall Street. But what a change! He was attired in a new suit, wore a fancy necktie, while a chain, that looked like gold, dangled from his watch pocket. Grant stared at him in amazement.

"How are you, Grant?" said Tom, patronizingly.

"Very well, thank you."

"I hope you are a-doin' well."

"Very well. You seem to be prosperous."

"Yes," answered Tom, languidly, evidently enjoying his surprise. "I told you I expected to get into something good. By the way, I owe you a quarter - there it is. Much obliged for the accommodation."

Grant pocketed the coin, which he had never expected to receive, and continued to regard Tom with puzzled surprise. He could not understand what business Tom could have found that had so altered his circumstances. He ventured to inquire.

"I wouldn't mind tellin' you," answered Tom, "but, you see, it's kind of confidential. I'm a confidential agent; that's it."

"It seems to be a pretty good business," remarked Grant.

"Yes, it is; I don't work for nothin', I can tell you that."

"I'm glad of your good luck, Tom," said Grant, and he spoke sincerely. "I hope you'll keep your agency."

"Oh, I guess I will! A feller like me is pretty sure of a good livin', anyway. Hello, Jim!"

This last was addressed to a flashily dressed individual - the same one, in fact, that Grant had seen on a former occasion with Tom.

"Who's your friend?" asked Jim, with a glance at Grant.

"Grant Thornton. He's from my place in the country. He's in the office of Mr. Reynolds, a broker in New Street."

"Introduce me."

"Grant, let me make you acquainted with my friend, Jim Morrison," said Tom, with a flourish.

"Glad to make your acquaintance, Mr. Thornton," said Jim Morrison, jauntily, offering his hand.

"Thank you," said Grant, in a reserved tone; for he was not especially attracted by the look of Tom's friend. He shook hands, however.

"Come 'round and see us some evenin', Grant," said Tom. "We'll take you round, won't we, Jim?"

"Of course we will. Your friend should see something of the city."

"You're the feller that can show him. Well, we must be

goin'. It's lunch time."

Tom pulled out a watch, which, if not gold, was of the same color as gold, and the two sauntered away.

"What in the world can Tom have found to do?" Grant wondered.

CHAPTER XIV

WILLIS FORD'S NEW FRIENDS

When Harry Decker left the office at the end of two weeks, Grant was fully able to take his place, having, with Harry's friendly assistance, completely mastered the usual routine of a broker's office. He had also learned the names and offices of prominent operators, and was, in all respects, qualified to be of service to his employer.

Mr. Reynolds always treated him with friendly consideration, and appeared to have perfect confidence in him. For some reason which he could not understand, however, Willis Ford was far from cordial, often addressing him in a fault-finding tone, which at first disturbed Grant. When he found that it arose from Ford's dislike, he ceased to trouble himself about it, though it annoyed him. He had discovered Ford's relationship to Mrs. Estabrook, who treated him in the same cool manner.

"As it appears I can't please them," Grant said to himself, "I won't make any special effort to do so." He contented himself with doing his work faithfully, and so satisfying his own conscience.

One evening some weeks later, Grant was returning

from a concert, to which the broker had given him a ticket, when, to his great surprise, he met Willis Ford walking with Tom Calder and Jim Morrison. The three were apparently on intimate terms.

"Good-evenin', Grant," said Tom.

"Good-evening, Tom."

Grant looked at Willis Ford, but the latter's lip curled and he did not speak. Grant, however, bowed and passed on. He was surprised at the intimacy which had grown up between Ford and those two, knowing Ford's spirit of exclusiveness. He would have been less surprised had he known that Morrison had first ingratiated himself with Ford by offering to lend him money, and afterward had lured him into a gambling house, where Ford, not knowing that he was a dupe, had been induced to play, and was now a loser to the extent of several hundred dollars, for which Morrison held his notes.

"I don't know when I can pay you," said Ford, gloomily, when he came to realize his situation.

"Oh, something will turn up." said Jim Morrison, lightly. "I shan't trouble you."

Two weeks later, however, he lay in wait for Ford when he left Wall Street.

"I want to speak to you a moment, Mr. Ford," he said.

"Well, what is it?" asked Ford, uncomfortably.

"I am hard up."

"So am I," responded Willis Ford.

"But you owe me a matter of six hundred dollars."

"I know it, but you said you wouldn't trouble me."

"I didn't expect I should be obliged to," said Morrison, smoothly. "But 'Circumstances alter cases,' you know. I shall have to ask you for it."

"That's all the good it will do," said Willis, irritably. "I haven't a cent to my name."

"When do you expect to have?"

"Heaven knows; I don't."

Ford was about to leave his companion and walk away, but Morrison had no intention of allowing the matter to end so. He laid his hand on Ford's shoulder and said, firmly: "Mr. Ford, this won't do. Yours is a debt of honor, and must be paid."

"Will you be kind enough to let me know how it is to be paid?" demanded Ford, with an ugly sneer.

"That is your business, not mine, Mr. Ford."

"Then, if it is my business, I'll give you notice when I can pay you. And now, good-afternoon."

He made another attempt to walk away, but again there was a hand placed upon his shoulder.

"Understand, Mr. Ford, that I am in earnest," said Morrison. "I can't undertake to tell you how you are to find the money, but it must be found."

"Suppose it isn't?" said Ford, with a look of defiance.

"Then I shall seek an interview with your respected employer, tell him of the debt, and how it was incurred, and I think he would look for another clerk."

"You wouldn't do that!" said Ford, his face betraying consternation.

"I would, and I will, unless you pay what you owe me."

"But, man, how am I to do it? You will drive me to desperation."

"Take three days to think of it. If you can't raise it, I may suggest a way."

The two parted, and Willis Ford was left to many uncomfortable reflections. He knew of no way to raise the money; yet, if he did not do it, he was menaced with exposure and ruin. Would his stepmother come to his assistance? He knew that Mrs. Estabrook had a thousand dollars in government bonds. If he could only induce her to give him the custody of them on any pretext, he could meet the demand upon him, and he would never again incur a debt of honor. He cursed his folly for ever yielding to the temptation. Once let him get out of this scrape, and he would never get into another like it.

The next evening he made a call upon Mrs. Estabrook, and made himself unusually agreeable. The cold-hearted woman, whose heart warmed to him alone, smiled upon him with affection.

"I am glad to see you in such good spirits, Willis," she said.

"If she only knew how I really felt," thought her stepson. But it was for his interest to wear a mask.

"The fact is, mother," he said, "I feel very cheerful. I've made a little turn in stocks, and realized three hundred dollars."

"Have you, indeed, Willis? I congratulate you, my son. No doubt you will find the money useful."

"No doubt of that. If I had the capital, I could make a good deal more."

"But there would be the danger of losing," suggested Mrs. Estabrook.

"That danger is very small, mother. I am in a situation to know all about the course of stocks. I wouldn't advise another to speculate, unless he has some friend in the Stock Exchange; but for me it is perfectly safe."

"Pray be careful, Willis."

"Oh, yes. I am sure to be. By the way, mother, haven't you got some money in government bonds?"

"A little," answered Mrs. Estabrook, cautiously.

"How much, now?"

"About a thousand dollars."

"Let me manage it for you, and I will make it two thousand inside of a month."

Mrs. Estabrook had a large share of acquisitiveness, but she had also a large measure of caution, which she had inherited from her Scotch ancestry.

"No, Willis," she said, shaking her head, "I can't take any risk. This money it has taken me years to save. It is the sole dependence I have for my old age, and I can't run the risk of losing it."

"But two thousand dollars will be better than one, mother. Just let me tell you what happened to a customer of ours: He had above five hundred dollars in the savings bank, drawing four per cent interest - only twenty dollars a year. He had a friend in the Stock Exchange who took charge of it, bought stocks judiciously on a margin, then reinvested, and now, after three months, how much do you think it amounts to?"

"How much?" asked the housekeeper, with interest.

"Six thousand five hundred dollars - just thirteen times as much!" answered Willis, glibly.

This story, by the way, was all a fabrication, intended to influence his stepmother. Mrs. Estabrook never doubted Ford's statement, but her instinctive caution saved her from falling into the trap.

"It looks tempting, Willis," she said, "but I don't dare to take the risk." Ford was deeply disappointed, but did not betray it.

"It is for you to decide," said he, carelessly, then drifted to other subjects.

Ten minutes later he pressed his hand upon his breast, while his features worked convulsively. "I believe I am sick," he said.

"What can I do for you, my dear son?" asked the housekeeper, in alarm.

"If you have a glass of brandy!" gasped Willis.

"I will go downstairs and get some," she said, hurriedly.

No sooner had she left the room than Willis sprang to his feet, locked the door, then went to the bureau, unlocked the upper drawer - he had a key in his pocket which fitted the lock and, thrusting in his hand, drew out a long envelope containing one five-hundred-dollar government bond and five bonds of one hundred dollars each, which he thrust into his side pocket. Then, closing the drawer, he unlocked the door of the room, and when his step-mother returned he threw himself back in his chair, groaning. He took the glass of brandy the housekeeper brought him, and, after a few minutes, professing himself much better, left the house.

"Saved!" he exclaimed, triumphantly. "Now I shall be all right again."

CHAPTER XV

AN ARTFUL TRAP

Willis Ford was anxious to get away. He feared that Mrs. Estabrook might go to the bureau and discover the loss before he got out of the house, which would make it awkward for him. Once out in the street, he breathed more freely. He had enough with him to pay his only debt, and give him four hundred dollars extra. It might be supposed he would feel some compunction at robbing his stepmother of her all. Whatever her faults, she was devoted to him. But Willis Ford had a hard, selfish nature, and the only thought that troubled him was the fear that he might be found out. Indeed, the housekeeper's suspicions would be likely to fall upon him unless they could be turned in some other direction. Who should it be? There came to him an evil suggestion which made his face brighten with relief and malicious joy. The new boy, Grant Thornton, was a member of the household. He probably had the run of the house. What more probable than that he should enter Mrs. Estabrook's chamber and search her bureau? This was the way Willis reasoned. He knew that his stepmother hated Grant, and would be very willing to believe anything against him. He would take care that suspicion should fall in that direction. He thought of a way to heighten that suspicion. What it was my readers will learn in due time.

The next day, at half-past eight o'clock in the morning, on his way down Broadway, Willis Ford dropped into the Grand Central Hotel, and walked through the reading room in the rear. Here sat Jim Morrison and Tom Calder, waiting for him by appointment.

Ford took a chair beside them.

"Good-morning," he said, cheerfully.

"Have you brought the money?" asked Morrison, anxiously.

"Hush! don't speak so loud," said Ford, cautiously. "We don't want everybody to know our business."

"All right," said Morrison, in a lower voice; "but have you brought it?"

"Yes."

"You're a trump!" said Morrison, his face expressing his joy.

"That is to say, I've brought what amounts to the same thing."

"If it's your note," said Morrison, with sharp disappointment, "I don't want it."

"It isn't a note. It's what will bring the money."

"What is it, then?"

"It's government bonds for six hundred dollars."

"I don't know anything about bonds," said Morrison. "Besides, the amount is more than six hundred dollars."

"These bonds are worth a hundred and twelve, amounting in all to six hundred and seventy-two dollars. That's forty more than I owe you. I won't make any account of that, however, as you will have to dispose of them."

"I may get into trouble," said Morrison, suspiciously. "Where did they come from?"

"That does not concern you," said Ford, haughtily. "Don't I give them to you?"

"But where did you get them?"

"That is my business. If you don't want them, say the word, and I'll take them back."

"And when will you pay the money?"

"I don't know," answered Ford, curtly.

"Maybe he'll sell 'em for us himself," suggested Tom Calder.

"Good, Tom! Why can't you sell 'em and give me the money? Then you can pay the exact sum and save the forty dollars."

"I don't choose to do so," said Ford. "It seems to me you are treating me in a very strange manner. I offer you more than I owe you, and you make no end of objections to receiving it."

"I am afraid I'll get into trouble if I offer the bonds for sale," said Morrison, doggedly. "I don't know anybody in the business except you."

"Yes, you do," said Ford, a bright idea occurring to him.

"Who?"

"You know the boy in our office."

"Grant Thornton?" said Tom.

"Yes, Grant Thornton. Manage to see him, and ask him to dispose of the bonds for you. He will bring them to our office, and I will dispose of them without asking any questions."

"First rate!" said Tom. "That'll do, won't it, Jim?"

"I don't see why it won't," answered Morrison, appearing satisfied.

"I would suggest that you see him some time today."

"Good! Hand over the bonds."

Willis Ford had already separated the bonds into two parcels, six hundred in one and four hundred in the other. The first of these he passed over to Jim Morrison.

"Put it into your pocket at once," he said. "We don't want anyone to see them. There is a telegraph boy looking at us."

"I'm going to see if it is all there," muttered Morrison; and he drew from the envelope the two bonds, and ascertained, by a personal inspection, that they were as represented.

"It's all right," he said.

"You might have taken my word for it," said Willis Ford, offended.

"In matters of business I take no one's word," chuckled the confidence man.

"I wonder what they're up to," said the little telegraph boy to himself. "I know one of them fellers is a gambler. Wonder who that feller with him is? Them must be gov'ment bonds."

Johnny Cavanagh was an observing boy, and mentally photographed upon his memory the faces of the entire group, though he never expected to see any of them again.

When Grant was hurrying through Wall Street about noon he came upon Tom Calder and Morrison.

"Hello, there, Grant," said Tom, placing his hand upon his shoulder.

"What's the matter, Tom? I'm in a hurry," said Grant.

"Jim Morrison's got a little business for you."

"What is it?"

"He wants you to sell gov'ment bonds for him."

"You'd better take them round to our office."

"I haven't got time," said Morrison. "Just attend to them, like a good fellow, and I'll give you a dollar for your trouble."

"How much have you got?"

"Six hundred - a five hundred and a one."

"Are they yours?"

"Yes; I've had 'em two years, but now I've got to raise money."

"What do you want for them?"

"Regular price, whatever it is."

"When will you call for the money?"

"Meet me at Fifth Avenue Hotel with it tomorrow morning at nine o'clock."

"I shall have to meet you earlier - say half-past eight."

"All right. Here's the bonds."

Grant put the envelope into his pocket, and hurried to the Exchange.

When he returned to the office he carried the bonds to Willis Ford.

"Mr. Ford," he said, "an acquaintance of mine handed them to me to be sold."

"Some one you know?" queried Ford.

"I know him slightly."

"Well, I suppose it's all right. I'll make out a check to your order, and you can collect the money at the bank."

Grant interposed no objection, and put the check in his pocket.

"The boy's fallen into the trap," said Willis to himself, exultantly, as he proceeded to enter the transaction on the books.

CHAPTER XVI

GRANT FALLS UNDER SUSPICION

In furtherance of his scheme to throw suspicion upon Grant, Willis Ford decided to make another call upon his stepmother the succeeding evening. It occurred to him that she might possibly connect his visit of the evening before with her loss, and he wished to forestall this.

"Is Mrs. Estabrook at home?" he asked of the servant.

"Yes, sir."

When the housekeeper made her appearance he carefully scrutinized her face. She was calm and placid, and it was clear that she had not discovered the abstraction of the bonds.

"I dare say you are surprised to see me so soon again," he commenced.

"I am always glad to see you, Willis," she said. "Come upstairs."

"What a pleasant room you have, mother!"

"Yes, I am very comfortable. Have you had any return

of your sickness?" she asked, anxiously.

"No, I have been perfectly well. By the way, mother, I have a special object in calling."

"What is it, Willis?"

"I want to speak to you about those bonds of yours. If you will only sell them out, and invest in Erie, I am sure you will make in six months a sum equal to several years interest."

"That may be, Willis, but I am very timid about taking a risk. Those bonds represent all the property I have."

Willis Ford's conscience pricked him a little, when he heard her speaking thus of the property he had so heartlessly stolen; but he did not show it in his manner.

"What is the date of your bonds, mother?" he asked.

"I don't know. Does that make any difference?"

"It makes some difference. Those that have longest to run are most valuable."

"I can easily tell," said the housekeeper, as she rose from her chair and opened the bureau drawer, in full confidence that the bonds were safe.

It was an exciting moment for Willis Ford, knowing the sad discovery that awaited her.

She put her hand in that part of the drawer where she supposed the bonds to be, and found nothing. A shade of anxiety overspread her face, and she searched hurriedly in other parts of the drawer.

"Don't you find them, mother?" asked Willis.

"It is very strange," said Mrs. Estabrook, half to herself.

"What is strange?"

"I always kept the bonds in the right-hand corner of this drawer."

"And you can't find them?"

"I have looked all over the drawer."

"You may have put them, by mistake, in one of the other drawers."

"Heaven grant it!" said Mrs. Estabrook, her face white with anxiety.

"Let me help you, mother," said Willis, rising.

She did not object, for her hands trembled with nervousness.

The other drawers were opened and were thoroughly searched, but, of course, the bonds were not found.

Mrs. Estabrook seemed near fainting.

"I have been robbed," she said. "I am ruined."

"But who could have robbed you?" asked Ford, innocently.

"I-don't-know. Oh, Willis! it was cruel!" and the poor woman burst into tears. "All these years I have been saving, and now I have lost all. I shall die in the poorhouse after all."

"Not while I am living, mother," said Willis. "But the bonds must be found. They must be mislaid."

"No, no! they are stolen. I shall never see them again."

"But who has taken them? Ha! I have an idea."

"What is it?" asked the housekeeper, faintly.

"That boy - Grant Thornton - he lives in the house, doesn't he?"

"Yes," answered Mrs. Estabrook, in excitement. "Do you think he can have robbed me?"

"What a fool I am! I ought to have suspected when -"

"When what?"

"When he brought some bonds to me to-day to sell."

"He did!" exclaimed Mrs. Estabrook; "what were they?"

"A five-hundred-dollar and a hundred-dollar bond."

"I had a five-hundred and five one-hundred-dollar bonds. They were mine - the young villain!"

"I greatly fear so, mother."

"You ought to have kept them, Willis. Oh! why didn't you? Where is the boy? I will see Mr. Reynolds at once."

"Wait a minute, till I tell you all I know. The boy said the bonds were handed to him by an acquaintance."

"It was a falsehood."

"Do you know the number of your bonds, mother?"

"Yes, I have them noted down, somewhere."

"Good! I took the number of those the boy gave me for sale."

Mrs. Estabrook found the memorandum. It was compared with one which Willis Ford brought with him, and the numbers were identical. Four numbers, of course, were missing from Ford's list.

"That seems pretty conclusive, mother. The young rascal has stolen your bonds, and offered a part of them for sale. It was certainly bold in him to bring them to our office. Is he in the house?"

"I'll go and see."

"And bring Mr. Reynolds with you, if you can find him."

In an excited state, scarcely knowing what she did, the housekeeper went downstairs and found both parties of whom she was in search in the same room. She poured out her story in an incoherent manner, inveighing against Grant as a thief.

When Grant, with some difficulty, understood what was the charge against him, he was almost speechless with indignation.

"Do you mean to say I stole your bonds?" he demanded.

"Yes, I do; and it was a base, cruel act."

"I agree with you in that, Mrs. Estabrook. It was base and cruel, but I had nothing to do with it."

"You dare to say that, when you brought the bonds to my son, Willis, to be sold to-day?"

"Is this true, Grant?" asked Mr. Reynolds. "Did you sell any bonds at the office to-day?"

"Yes, sir."

The broker looked grave.

"Where did you get them?" he asked.

"They were handed to me by an acquaintance in Wall Street."

"Who was he?"

"His name is James Morrison."

"What do you know of him? Is he in any business?"

"I know very little of him, sir."

"Have you handed him the money?"

"No, sir. I am to meet him to-morrow morning at the Fifth Avenue Hotel, and pay him."

"Why doesn't he call at the office?"

"I don't know," answered Grant, puzzled. "I suggested to him to bring the bonds to the office himself, but he said he was in haste, and offered me a dollar to attend to the matter."

"This seems a mysterious case."

"Excuse me, Mr. Reynolds, but I think it is plain enough," said the housekeeper, spitefully. "That boy opened my bureau drawer, and stole the bonds."

"That is not true, Mr. Reynolds," exclaimed Grant, indignantly.

"How did you know the bonds were offered for sale at my office to-day, Mrs.Estabrook?" inquired the broker.

"My son - Willis Ford - told me."

"When did you see him?"

"Just now."

"Is he in the house?"

"Yes, sir. I left him in my room."

"Ask him to be kind enough to accompany you here."

The housekeeper left the room. Grant and his employer remained silent during her absence.

CHAPTER XVII

THE TELLTALE KEY

Willis Ford entered the presence of his employer with an air of confidence which he did not feel. Knowing his own guilt, he felt ill at ease and nervous; but the crisis had come and he must meet it.

"Take a seat, Mr. Ford," said Mr. Reynolds, gravely. "Your stepmother tells me that she has lost some government bonds?"

"All I had in the world," moaned the housekeeper.

"Yes, sir; I regret to say that she has been robbed."

"I learn, moreover, that a part of the bonds were brought to my office for sale to-day?"

"Yes, sir."

"And by Grant Thornton?"

"He can answer that question for himself, sir. He is present."

"It is true," said Grant, quietly.

"Did you ask him where the bonds came from?"

"He volunteered the information. He said they were intrusted to him for sale by a friend."

"Acquaintance," corrected Grant.

"It may have been so. I understood him to say friend."

"You had no suspicions that anything was wrong?" asked the broker.

"No; I felt perfect confidence in the boy."

Grant was rather surprised to hear this. If this were the case, Willis Ford had always been very successful, in concealing his real sentiments.

"How did you pay him?"

"In a check to his own order."

"Have you collected the money on that check, Grant?" asked Mr. Reynolds.

"Yes, sir."

"Have you paid it out to the party from whom you obtained the bonds?"

"No, sir; I am to meet him to-morrow morning at the Fifth Avenue Hotel."

Willis Ford's countenance changed when he heard this statement. He supposed that Jim Morrison already had his money and was safely off with it. Now it was clear that Grant would not be allowed to pay it to him, and his own debt would remain unpaid. That being the case, Morrison would be exasperated, and there was no knowing what he would say.

"What do you know of this man, Grant?"

"Very little, sir."

"How does he impress you - as an honest, straight-forward man?"

Grant shook his head.

"Not at all," he said.

"Yet you took charge of his business for him?"

"Yes, sir; but not willingly. He offered me a dollar for my trouble, and as I did not know there was anything wrong, I consented. Besides -" Here Grant paused.

"Well?"

"Will you excuse my continuing, Mr. Reynolds?"

"No," answered the broker, firmly. "On the other hand, I insist upon your saying what you had in your mind."

"Having seen Mr. Ford in this man's company, I concluded he was all right."

Willis Ford flushed and looked disconcerted.

"Is this true, Mr. Ford?" asked the broker. "Do you know this man?"

"What do you say his name was, Thornton?" asked Ford, partly to gain time.

"James Morrison."

"Yes; I know him. He was introduced to me by an intimate friend of that boy," indicating Grant.

Willis Ford smiled triumphantly. He felt that he had checkmated our hero.

"Is this true, Grant?"

"I presume so," answered Grant, coolly. "You refer to Tom Calder, do you not, Mr. Ford?"

"I believe that is his name."

"He is not an intimate friend of mine, but we came from the same village. It is that boy who was with me when I first met you, Mr. Reynolds."

The broker's face cleared.

"Yes, I remember him. But how do you happen to know Tom Calder, Mr. Ford?"

"He had a room at the same house with me. He introduced himself as a friend of this boy."

"Do you know anything of him - how he earns his living?"

"Haven't the faintest idea," answered Ford. "My acquaintance with him is very slight."

"There seems a mystery here," said the broker. "This Morrison gives Grant two bonds to dispose of, which are identified as belonging to my housekeeper. How did he obtain possession of them? That is the question."

"There isn't much doubt about that," said Mrs. Estabrook. "This boy whom you have taken into your family has taken them."

"You are entirely mistaken, Mrs. Estabrook," said Grant, indignantly.

"Of course you say so!" retorted the housekeeper; "but it stands to reason that that is the way it happened. You took them and gave them to this man - that is, if there is such a man."

"Your son says there is, Mrs. Estabrook," said the broker, quietly.

"Well, I don't intend to say how it happened. Likely enough the man is a thief, and that boy is his accomplice."

"You will oblige me by not jumping at conclusions, Mrs. Estabrook," said Mr. Reynolds. "Whoever has taken the bonds is likely to be discovered. Meanwhile your loss will, at all events, be partially made up, since Grant has the money realized from the sale of the greater part of them."

"I should like to place the money in your hands, Mr. Reynolds," said Grant.

"But it belongs to me," said the housekeeper.

"That is undoubtedly true," said her employer; "but till the matter is ascertained beyond a doubt I will retain the money."

"How can there be any doubt?" asked the housekeeper, discontented.

"I do not think there is; but I will tell you now. You claim that your bonds were marked by certain numbers, two of which belong to those which were bought by Mr. Ford at the office to-day?"

"Yes, sir."

"Meanwhile, you and your stepson have had time to compare notes, and you have had a chance to learn his numbers."

Mrs. Estabrook turned livid.

"I didn't expect to have such a charge brought against me, Mr. Reynolds, and by you," she said, her voice trembling with passion.

"I have brought no such charge, Mrs. Estabrook. I have only explained how there may be doubt of your claim to the money."

"I thought you knew me better, sir."

"I think I do, and I also think I know Grant better than to think him capable of abstracting your bonds. Yet you have had no hesitation in bringing this serious charge against him."

"That is different, sir."

"Pardon me, I can see no difference. He has the same right that you have to be considered innocent till he is proved to be guilty."

"You must admit, sir," said Willis Ford, "that appearances are very much against Grant."

"I admit nothing, at present; for the affair seems to be complicated. Perhaps, Mr. Ford, you can offer some suggestion that will throw light upon the mystery."

"I don't think it very mysterious, sir. My mother kept her bonds in the upper drawer of her bureau. This boy had the run of the house. What was to prevent his entering my mother's room, opening the drawer, and taking anything he found of value?"

"What was to prevent some one else doing it, Mr. Ford - myself, for example?"

"Of course that is different, Mr. Reynolds."

"Well, I don't know. I am honest, and so, I believe, is Grant."

"Thank you, sir," said Grant, gratefully.

"It just occurred to me," said Ford, "to ask my mother if she has at any time lost or mislaid her keys."

"Well thought of, Mr. Ford," and Mr. Reynolds turned to his housekeeper for a reply.

"No," answered Mrs. Estabrook. "I keep my keys in my pocket, and I have them there yet."

So saying, she produced four keys attached to a ring.

"Then," continued Ford, "if Grant chances to have a key which will fit the bureau drawer, that would be evidence against him."

"Show me any keys you may have, Grant," said the broker.

Grant thrust his hand in his pocket and drew out two keys. He looked at them in astonishment.

"One of them unlocks my valise," he said. "The other is a strange key. I did not know I had it."

Ford smiled maliciously. "Let us see if it will open the bureau drawer," he said.

The party adjourned to the housekeeper's room. The key was put into the lock of the bureau drawer and opened it at once.

"I think there is no more to be said," said Willis Ford, triumphantly.

Grant looked the picture of surprise and dismay.

CHAPTER XVIII

GRANT'S ENEMIES TRIUMPH

It is not too much to say that Grant was overwhelmed by the unexpected discovery, in his pocket, of a key that fitted the housekeeper's drawer. He saw at once how strong it made the evidence against him, and yet he knew himself to be innocent. The most painful thought was, that Mr. Reynolds would believe him to be guilty.

In fact, the broker for the first time began to think that Grant might possibly have yielded to temptation.

"Can't you account for the possession of that key?" he asked.

"No, sir," answered Grant, in painful embarrassment. "I have occasion to use but one key, and that is the key to my valise."

"I think you had occasion to use the other," sneered Ford.

"Mr. Ford," retorted Grant, indignantly, "you are determined to think me guilty; but I care nothing for your opinion. I should be very sorry if Mr. Reynolds should think me capable of such baseness."

"Your guilt seems pretty clear," said Ford, sarcastically; "as I have no doubt Mr. Reynolds will agree."

"Speak for yourself, Mr. Ford," said the banker, quietly.

"I hope you are not going to shield that young thief, Mr. Reynolds," said the housekeeper. "His guilt is as clear as noonday. I think he ought to be arrested."

"You are rather in a hurry, Mrs. Estabrook," said Mr. Reynolds; "and I must request you to be careful how you make charges against me."

"Against you?" asked the housekeeper, alarmed at his tone.

"Yes," answered the broker, sternly. "You have insinuated that I intend to shield a supposed thief. I have only to say that at present the theft is to be proved."

"I submit, sir," said Ford, "that the evidence is pretty strong. The boy is proved to have had the bonds in his possession, he admits that he sold a part of them and has the money in his possession, and a key is found in his possession which will open the drawer in which the bonds were kept."

"Who put the key in my pocket?" demanded Grant, quickly.

For a moment Willis Ford looked confused, and his momentary confusion was not lost upon Grant or the banker.

"No doubt you put it there yourself," he answered, sharply, after a monent's pause.

"That matter will be investigated," said the broker.

"I think the money ought to be paid to me," said the housekeeper.

"Can you prove your ownership of the bonds?" asked the broker.

"I can," answered Willis Ford, flippantly. "I have seen them."

"I should like some additional evidence," said Mr. Reynolds. "You are related to Mrs. Esta-brook, and may be supposed to have some interest in the matter."

"What proof can I have?" asked the housekeeper, disturbed by this unexpected obstacle.

"Have you the memorandum of the broker who bought you the bonds."

"I don't know, sir."

"Then you had better look."

The housekeeper searched the drawer, and produced, triumphantly, a memorandum to the effect that she had purchased the bonds of a well-known house in Wall Street.

"So far, so good!" said the broker. "It appears that besides the bonds sold you had four one-hundred-dollar bonds?"

"Yes, sir."

"You had not parted with them?"

"No, sir."

"They will some time be put on the market, and then we shall have a clew to the mystery."

"That boy has probably got them," said the housekeeper, nodding her head emphatically.

"You are at liberty to search my chamber, Mrs. Estabrook," said Grant, quietly.

"He may have passed them over to that man Morrison," suggested the housekeeper.

"I hardly think that likely," said Willis Ford, who saw danger to himself in any persecution of Jim Morrison.

Mr. Reynolds noticed his defense of Morrison, and glanced at him thoughtfully.

"Mrs. Estabrook," he said, "I am satisfied that you possessed the bonds which you claim, and I will relieve your mind by saying that I will guarantee you against loss by their disappearance. You need have no further anxiety on the subject. I will undertake to investigate the matter, which at present appears to be involved in mystery. Whether or not I succeed in solving it will not matter to you, since you are saved from loss."

"Thank you, sir," said the housekeeper, feeling considerably relieved; "it wasn't much, but it was my all. I depended upon it to use when old age prevented me from earning my living."

"I am glad you are so wise in providing for the future."

"You won't let that boy escape?" the housekeeper could not help adding.

"If you refer to Grant Thornton, I think I may say for him that he has no intention of leaving us."

"Is he to stay in the house?"

"Of course; and I expect him to aid me in coming to the truth. Let me request, Mrs. Estabrook, that you discontinue referring to him in offensive terms, or I may withdraw my offer guaranteeing you from loss. Grant, if you will accompany me, I have some questions to put to you."

Grant and his employer left the room together.

"He won't let the boy be punished, though he must know he's guilty," said Mrs. Estabrook, spitefully.

"He makes a fool of himself about that boy," said Willis Ford, disconcerted.

"He's an artful young vagabond," said the housekeeper. "I know he took the bonds."

"Of course he did," Ford assented, though he had the best of reasons for knowing that Grant was innocent.

"At any rate," he continued, "you are all right, mother, since Mr. Reynolds agrees to make up the value of the bonds to you. When you get your money, just consult me about investing it. Don't put it into bonds, for they may be stolen."

"Perhaps I'd better put it into the savings bank," said his stepmother.

"You'll get very small interest there; I can invest it so you can make quite as much. However, there will be time enough to speak of that when you've got the money. Now, mother, I shall have to bid you good-evening."

"Can't you stay longer, Willis? I feel so upset that I don't like to be left alone. I don't know what that boy may do."

"I think you are safe," said Willis Ford, secretly amused. But, as he left the house, he felt seriously disquieted. There was danger that Jim Morrison, when he found the money which he was to receive withheld, would be incensed and denounce Ford, who had received back his evidence of indebtedness. Should he divulge that the bonds had been given him by Ford, Grant would be cleared, and he would be convicted of theft.

As Ford was leaving the house a telegraph boy was just ascending the steps. It was John Cava-nagh, already referred to.

As his eyes rested on Ford, he said to himself: "Where have I seen that feller? I know his face."

Then it flashed upon the boy that he had seen Ford at the Grand Central Hotel, in the act of giving bonds to

Jim Morrison.

"It's queer I should meet him here," said the telegraph boy to himself. "I wonder what game he's up to."

Johnny was introduced into the presence of Mr. Reynolds, for whom he had a message. On his way out he met Grant in the hall. The two boys were acquainted, Grant having at one time advanced Johnny two dollars toward paying his mother's rent.

"Do you live here?" asked the telegraph boy.

"Yes," answered Grant.

"I met a feller goin' out that I've seen before. Who was it?"

"Willis Ford, a clerk of Mr. Reynolds."

"I seed him in the Grand Central Hotel yesterday givin' some bonds to a suspicious-lookin' chap."

"You did," exclaimed Grant. "Come right up and tell that to Mr. Reynolds," and he seized the astonished telegraph boy by the arm.

CHAPTER XIX

IMPORTANT EVIDENCE

Mr. Reynolds looked rather surprised when Grant appeared, drawing the telegraph boy after him.

"This boy has got something to tell you about Mr. Ford," said Grant, breathless with excitement.

"About Mr. Ford?" repeated the broker. "What do you know about Willis Ford?"

"I don't know his name," replied Johnny. "It's the chap that just went out of the house."

"It was Mr. Ford," explained Grant.

"Tell me what you know about him," said the broker, encouragingly.

"I seed him in the Grand Central Hotel, givin' some bond to a flashy-lookin' man. There was a boy wid him, a big boy."

"With whom - Mr. Ford?"

"No, wid the other chap."

"I know who he means, sir," said Grant. "It was Tom Calder."

"And the man?"

"Was Jim Morrison, the same man that gave me the bonds to sell."

"That seems important," said Mr. Reynolds. "I did not believe Ford capable of such rascality."

"He had as good a chance to take the bonds as I, sir. He was here last evening."

"Was he?" asked the broker, quickly. "I did not know that."

"He was here for an hour at least. I saw him come in and go out."

Mr. Reynolds asked several more questions of the telegraph boy, and enjoined him to silence.

"My boy," he said, "come here to-rnorrow evening at half-past seven. I may want you."

"I will, sir, if I can get away. I shall be on duty."

"Say to the telegraph company that I have an errand for you. Your time will be paid for."

"That will make it all right, sir."

"And, meanwhile, here is a dollar for your own use."

Johnny's eyes sparkled, for with his limited earnings

this sum would come in very handy. He turned away, nearly forgetting the original errand that brought him to the house, but luckily it occurred in time. The nature of it has nothing to do with this story.

When Johnny had gone, Mr. Reynolds said: "Grant, I need not caution you not to breathe a word of this. I begin to think that there is a conspiracy against you; but whether Willis Ford is alone in it, or has a confederate I cannot decide. My housekeeper does not appear to like you."

"No, sir, I am sorry to say she does not; but I don't think she is in this plot. I think she honestly believes that I stole her bonds."

"I have too great confidence in you to believe it. I own I was a little shaken when the key was found. You have no idea how it came in your pocket, I suppose?"

"No, sir, I can't guess. I might suspect Mr. Ford of putting it there, but I can't see how he managed it."

"Well, we will let matters take their course. You will go to work as usual, and not speak a word of what has happened this evening."

"Thank you, sir."

Meanwhile, we must follow Willis Ford. When he left the house, he was by no means in a comfortable frame of mind. He felt that it was absolutely necessary to see Jim Morrison, and have an understanding with him. What arrangements he could make with him, or how he could reconcile him to the loss of the money which he had expected to receive from the sale of the bonds, he could not yet imagine. Perhaps he would be willing to receive the other four bonds in part payment. In that case Willis himself would not profit as much as he had hoped from the theft; but there seemed no alternative. He had got himself into a scrape, and he must get out of it the best way possible.

Though he did not know where to find Morrison, he thought it likely that he might be seen at the White Elephant, a large and showy billiard room on Broadway, near Thirtieth Street. There were several gambling houses near by, and there or in that neighborhood he thought that Morrison might be met.

He was right. On entering the billiard room he found the man he sought playing a game of billiards with Tom Calder, at the first table.

"I want to see you, Morrison," he said, in a low voice. "Is the game 'most finished?"

"I have only six points more to make. I shall probably run out this time."

He was right in his estimate. Two minutes later the two went out of the saloon together, accompanied by Tom.

"Well, what is it?" he asked.

"Let us turn into a side street."

They turned into Thirtieth Street, which was much less brilliantly lighted than Broadway, and sauntered leisurely along.

"Did you buy the bonds of that boy?" asked Morrison, anxiously.

"Yes."

"Then it's all right. Have you brought me the money?"

"How should I?" returned Ford, impatiently. "I couldn't pay him, and keep the money myself."

"Oh, well, it doesn't matter. He is to meet me to-morrow morning and hand over the money."

"I am afraid you will be disappointed." "Disapp-ointed," repeated Morrison, quickly. "What do you mean? The boy hasn't made off with the money, has he? If he has -" and the sentence ended with an oath.

"No, it isn't as you suppose."

"Then why won't he pay me the money, I'd like to know?"

"There is some trouble about the bonds. It is charged that they are stolen."

"How is that? You gave them to me," said Morrison, suspiciously.

Now came the awkward moment. However, Ford had decided on the story he would tell.

"They were given me by a person who owed me money," he said, plausibly. "How was I to know they were stolen?"

"They were stolen, then?"

"I suppose so. In fact, I know so."

"How do you know?"

"Well - in fact, they were stolen from my stepmother."

Morrison whistled.

"Well," he said.

"Of course you mustn't say that I gave them to you. You would get me into trouble."

"So you want to save yourself at my expense? I am to be suspected of stealing the bonds, am I? That's a decidedly cool proposal, but it won't do. I shall clear myself, by telling just where I got the bonds."

"That's what I want you to do."

"You do!" ejaculated the gambler, in surprise.

"Yes. You are to say that the boy gave them to you."

"Why should I say that?"

"Because he is already suspected of stealing the bonds."

"But I gave them to him to sell."

"You mustn't admit it. There is no proof of it except his word."

"What's your game? Whatever it is, it is too deep for me."

"I've got it all arranged. You are to say that the boy owed you a gambling debt, and agreed to meet you to-morrow morning to pay it. Of the bonds, you are to know nothing, unless you say that he told you he had some which he was going to sell, in order to get money to pay you."

"What advantage am I to get out of all this?"

"What advantage? Why, you will save yourself from suspicion."

"That isn't enough. I didn't take the bonds, and you know it. I believe you did it yourself."

"Hush!" said Willis Ford, looking around him nervously.

"Look here, Ford, I gave up your I O U, and now I find I've got to whistle for my money."

"Go with me to my room, and you shall have four hundred dollars to-night."

"In cash?"

"No; in bonds."

"Some more of the same kind? No, thank you, I want ready money."

"Then give me a little more time, and I will dispose of them - when this excitement blows over."

Finally Morrison gave a sulky assent, and the conspirators parted.

CHAPTER XX

AT THE FIFTH AVENUE HOTEL

"If I thought he was playing me false," said Jim Morrison, after Ford and himself had parted company, "I'd make him smart for it."

"I guess it's all right," said Tom, who was less experienced and less suspicious than his companion.

"It may be so, but I have my suspicions. I don't trust Willis Ford."

"Shall you go round to the Fifth Avenue Hotel to meet Grant to-morrow morning."

"Of course I shall. I want to see what the boy says. It may be a put-up job between him and Ford."

The very same question was put by Grant to Mr. Reynolds.

"Shall I go round to the hotel to-morrow morning to see Morrison and Tom Calder?"

The broker paused a moment and looked thoughtful.

"Yes," he answered, after a pause. "You may."

"And what shall I say when he demands the money?"

Upon this Mr. Reynolds gave Grant full instructions as to what he desired him to say.

About quarter after eight o'clock the next morning a quiet-looking man, who looked like a respectable bookkeeper entered the Fifth Avenue Hotel and walked through the corridor, glancing, as it seemed, indifferently, to the right and. left. Finally he reached the door of the reading room and entered. His face brightened as at the further end he saw two persons occupying adjoining seats. They were, in fact, Morrison and Tom Calder.

The newcomer selected a Boston daily paper, and, as it seemed, by chance, settled himself in a seat not six feet away from our two acquaintances, so that he could, without much effort, listen to their conversation.

"It's almost time for Grant to come," said Tom, after a pause.

"Yes," grumbled Morrison, "but as he won't have any money for me, I don't feel as anxious as I should otherwise."

"What'll you say to him?"

"I don't know yet. I want to find out whether Ford has told the truth about the bonds. I believe he stole 'em himself."

Five minutes later Grant entered the reading-room. A quick glance showed him, not only the two he had come to meet, but the quiet, little man who was apparently absorbed in a copy of the Boston Journal. He went up at once to meet them.

"I believe I am in time," he said.

"Yes," answered Jim Morrison. "Have you brought the money?"

"No."

"Why not?" demanded Morrison, with a frown.

"There was something wrong about the bonds you gave me to sell."

"Weren't they all right? They weren't counterfeit, were they?"

"They were genuine, but -"

"But what?"

"A lady claims that they belong to her - that they were stolen from her. Of course you can explain how they came into your hands?"

"They were given me by a party that owed me money. If he's played a trick on me, it will be the worse for him. Did you sell them?"

"Yes."

"Then give me the money."

"Mr. Reynolds won't let me."

"Does he think I took the bonds?" asked Morrison, hastily.

"No, he doesn't," answered Grant, proudly, "but he would like to have an interview with you, and make some inquiries, so that he may form some idea as to the person who did take them. They belonged to his housekeeper, Mrs. Estabrook, who is the stepmother of Mr. Ford, a young man employed in our office."

Tom Calder and Jim Morrison exchanged glances. Grant's story agreed with Ford's, and tended to confirm their confidence in his good faith.

"When does he want to see me?" asked Morrison.

"Can you call at his house this evening at eight o'clock?"

"Where does he live?"

Grant mentioned the street and number.

"I will be there," he said, briefly.

"Can I come, too?" asked Tom Calder, addressing the question to Grant.

"There will be no objection, I think."

"Tell him we'll be on hand."

The three left the hotel together, Grant taking a Broadway stage at the door. The quiet man seemed no longer interested in the Boston Journal, for he hung it up in its place, and sauntered out of the hotel. He had not attracted the attention of Jim Morrison or Tom.

When Grant entered the office, and with his usual manner asked Ford if he should go to the post-office, the young man eyed him curiously.

"Are you to remain in the office?" he said.

"Yes, I suppose so."

"After what you have done?"

"What have I done, Mr. Ford?" asked Grant, eyeing the young man, steadily.

"I don't think you need to have me tell you," he said, with a sneer. "I don't think Mr. Reynolds is very prudent to employ a boy convicted of dishonesty."

"Do you believe me guilty, Mr. Ford?" asked our hero, calmly.

"The evidence against you is overwhelming. My mother ought to have you arrested."

"The person who stole the bonds may be arrested."

"What do you mean?" asked Willis Ford, flushing, and looking disconcerted.

"I mean that I have no concern in the matter. Shall I go to the post-office?"

"Yes," snapped Ford, "and take care you don't steal any of the letters."

Grant did not reply. He knew that his vindication was certain, and he was willing to wait.

If Willis Ford had been prudent he would have dropped the matter there, but his hatred of Grant was too great to be easily concealed. When a few minutes later the broker entered the office and inquired, "Where is Grant?" Ford, after answering, "he has gone to the post-office," could not help saying, "Are you going to keep that boy, Mr. Rey-nolds?"

"Why should I not?" the broker replied.

"I thought a boy in his position ought to be honest."

"I agree with you, Mr. Ford," said the broker, quietly.

"After taking my mother's bonds, that can hardly be said of Grant Thornton."

"You seem to be sure he did take them, Mr. Ford."

"The discovery of the key settled that to my mind."

"Grant says he has no knowledge of the key."

Ford laughed scornfully.

"Of course he would say so," he replied.

"I propose to investigate the matter further," said the broker. "Can you make it convenient to call at my house this evening? Possibly something may be discovered by that time."

"Yes, sir; I will come, with pleasure. I have no feeling

in regard to the boy, except that I don't think it safe to employ him in a business like yours."

"I agree with you, Mr. Ford. One who is capable of stealing bonds from a private house is unfit to be employed in an office like mine."

"Yet you retain the boy, sir?"

"For the present. It is not fair to assume that he is guilty till we have demonstrated it beyond a doubt."

"I think there will be no difficulty about that, Mr. Reynolds," said Willis Ford, well pleased at these words.

"I sincerely hope that his innocence may be proved."

Soon afterward Mr. Reynolds went to the Stock Exchange, and Willis Ford returned to his routine duties.

"With the testimony of Jim Morrison I shall be able to fix you, my young friend," he said to himself, as Grant returned from the post-office.

No further allusion was made to the matter during the day. Grant and Willis Ford were both looking forward to the evening, but for different reasons. Grant expected to be vindicated, while Ford hoped he could convince the broker of the boy's guilt.

CHAPTER XXI

THE THIEF IS DISCOVERED

Willis Ford ascended the steps of the broker's residence with a jaunty step. The servant admitted him, but he met Grant in the hall.

"Won't you come upstairs, Mr. Ford?" he said.

Willis Ford nodded superciliously.

"Your stay in the house will be short, young man," he thought. "You had better make the most of it."

He was ushered not into the housekeeper's room, but into a sitting-room on the second floor. He found Mr. Reynolds and his stepmother there already. Both greeted him, the broker gravely, but his stepmother cordially. Grant did not come in.

"I have come as you requested, Mr. Reynolds," he said. "I suppose it's about the bonds. May I ask if you have discovered anything new?"

"I think I have," answered the broker, slowly.

The housekeeper looked surprised. If anything new had been discovered, she at least had not heard it.

"May I ask what it is?" Ford inquired, carelessly.

"You shall know in good time. Let me, however, return the question. Have you heard anything calculated to throw light on the mystery?"

"No, sir, I can't say I have. To my mind there is no mystery at all about the affair."

"I presume I understand what you mean. Still I will ask you to explain yourself."

"Everything seems to throw suspicion upon that boy, Grant Thornton. Nobody saw him take the bonds, to be sure, but he has had every opportunity of doing so, living in the same house, as he does. Again, a key has been found in his pocket, which will open the bureau drawer in which the bonds were kept; and, thirdly, I can testify, and the boy admits, that he presented them at our office for sale, and received the money for them. I think, sir, that any jury would consider this accumulation of proof conclusive."

"It does seem rather strong," said the broker, gravely. "I compliment you on the way you have summed up, Mr. Ford."

Willis Ford looked much gratified. He was susceptible to flattery, and he was additionally pleased, because, as he thought, Mr. Reynolds was impressed by the weight of evidence.

"I have sometimes thought," he said, complacently, "that I ought to have become a lawyer. I always had a liking for the profession."

"Still," said the broker, deliberately, "we ought to consider Grant's explanation of the matter. He says that the bonds were intrusted to him for sale by a third party."

"Of course he would say something like that," returned Willis, shrugging his shoulders. "He can hardly expect anyone to be taken in by such a statement as that."

"You think, then, that he had no dealings with this Morrison?"

"I don't say that, sir," said Ford, remembering the story which he and Morrison had agreed upon. It may be stated here that he had been anxious to meet Morrison before meeting the coming appointment, in order to ascertain what had passed between him and Grant. With this object in view, he had gone to the usual haunts of the gambler, but had been unable to catch sight of him. However, as he had seen him the evening previous, and agreed upon the story to be told, he contented himself with that.

"You think, then, that Morrison may have given Grant the bonds?" said Mr. Reynolds.

"No, sir; that is not my idea."

"Have you any other notion?"

"I think the boy may have been owing him money, and took this method of raising it."

"But how should he owe him money?" asked the broker, curiously.

"I don't wish to say anything against Morrison, but I have been told that he is a gambler. Grant may have lost money to him at play."

"Or you," thought the broker; but he said:

"Your suggestion is worth considering, but I don't think Grant has had any opportunity to lose money in that way, as he spends his evenings usually at home."

"It wouldn't take long to lose a great deal of money, sir."

"That explains it," said the housekeeper, speaking for the first time. "I have no doubt Willis is right, and the boy gambles."

"I presume, Mr. Ford," said the broker, with a peculiar look, "that you do not approve of gambling?"

"Most certainly not, sir," said Ford, his face expressing the horror which a so-well-conducted young man must naturally feel for so pernicious a habit.

"I am glad to hear it. Will you excuse me a moment?"

After the broker had left the room, Mrs. Estabrook turned to Willis and said: "You are pretty sharp, Willis. You have found out this wretched boy, and now I think we shall get rid of him."

"I flatter myself, mother," said Willis, complacently, "that I have given the old man some new ideas as to the character of his favorite. I don't think we shall see him in the office again."

As he spoke, his ears caught the sound of ascending footsteps on the stairs without. He was rather puzzled. He conjectured that Grant had been summoned to confront his accuser, but there seemed, from the sound, to be more than two approaching. When the door opened, and the broker gravely ushered in Jim Morrison and Tom Calder, both looking ill at ease, followed by Grant Thornton, he looked amazed and perplexed.

"I believe you know these gentlemen," said Mr. Reynolds, gravely. "I have thought it best to make our present investigation thorough and complete."

"I have met the gentlemen before," said Ford, uncomfortably.

"You also have met them, Grant, have you not?"

"Yes, sir."

"Have you had any business transaction with either?"

"Yes, sir. Mr. Morrison met me on Wall Street and handed me two bonds, with a request that I would sell them for him, and hand him the money the next morning, at the Fifth Avenue Hotel."

"Were these the same bonds that you sold to Mr. Ford?"

"Yes, sir."

"I think the boy is lying, sir," burst out Ford.

"What have you to say to the boy's story, Mr.

Morrison?" asked the broker.

"He's made a little mistake," answered Jim Morrison, who by this time was feeling more at his ease. "I didn't give him no bonds."

Willis Ford looked triumphant, and Grant amazed.

"How, then, could there be any business between you?"

"I may as well own up that I am a gambler," replied Morrison, with virtuous frankness. "The boy lost the money to me at play, and said he'd meet and pay me at the Fifth Avenue Hotel. I didn't know where he was goin' to get the money, but I expect he must have stolen the bonds, and got it that way."

Considering the damaging nature of the revelation, Grant showed considerable self-command. He did not turn pale, nor did he look guilty and conscience-stricken.

"What have you to say to this charge, Grant?" asked the broker.

"It is not true, sir."

"What a hardened young villain!" said the house-keeper, in a low, but audible voice.

"Mr. Reynolds will hardly believe you," said Ford, turning upon our hero and speaking in a tone of virtuous indignation. "You see, sir," he continued, addressing the broker, "that I was right in my conjecture."

"I am not quite satisfied yet," said Mr. Reynolds. "Grant, call the boy."

Great was the perplexity of Willis Ford and his friends when Grant left the room, and almost immediately reappeared with a small boy in blue uniform. Not one of them recognized him.

"Have you ever seen any of these gentlemen before, my boy?" asked the broker.

"I've seed 'em all, sir," answered the boy.

"State where you saw them last."

"I seed him, and him, and him," said Johnny, pointing out Willis Ford, Jim Morrison and Tom Calder, "at the Grand Central Hotel yesterday mornm'."

Ford started and became very pale.

"What passed between them?"

"He," indicating Ford, "gave some bonds to him," indicating Morrison, "and got back a bit of paper. I don't know what was on it."

"It is false!" ejaculated Willis Ford, hoarsely.

CHAPTER XXII

WILLIS FORD AT BAY

The telegraph boy's evidence overwhelmed Willis Ford and his confederates with dismay. The feeling was greater in Ford, for it tended to fasten the theft upon him, while Jim Morrison and Tom Calder, though convicted of falsehood, were at all events sustained by the consciousness that nothing worse could be alleged against them.

"It is false!" asserted Willis Ford, with a flushed face.

"It is true!" declared the telegraph boy, sturdily.

"I don't believe a word of it," said the housekeeper, angrily.

"This is a startling revelation, Mr. Ford," said the broker, gravely.

"It is a base conspiracy, sir," returned Ford, hoarsely. "I submit, sir, that the word of a boy like that ought not to weigh against mine. Besides, these gentlemen," indicating Jim Morrison and Tom Calder, "will corroborate my statement."

"Of course we do," blustered Morrison. "That boy

is a liar!"

"I have spoken the truth, sir, and they know it," asserted Johnny, resolutely.

"How much did Grant Thornton pay you for telling this lie?" demanded Willis Ford, furiously.

"I will answer that question, Mr. Ford," said Grant, thinking it time to speak for himself. "I paid him nothing, and did not know till last evening that he had witnessed the interview between you and Mr. Morrison."

"Your word is of no value," said Ford, scornfully.

"That is a matter for Mr. Reynolds to consider," answered Grant, with composure.

"Mr. Ford," said the broker, gravely, "I attach more importance to the testimony of this telegraph boy than you appear to; but then it is to be considered that you are an interested party."

"Am I to be discredited on account of what a wretched telegraph boy chooses to say?" asked Ford, bitterly. "Even supposing him worthy of credence, my two friends sustain me, and it is three against one."

"They are your friends, then?" asked Mr. Reynolds, significantly.

Willis Ford flushed. It was not to his credit to admit that an acknowledged gambler was his friend, yet he knew that to deny it would make Morrison angry, and perhaps lead him to make some awkward revelations.

"I have not known them long, sir," he answered, embarrassed, "but I believe they feel friendly to me. One of them," he added, maliciously, "is an old friend of Grant Thornton."

"Yes," answered Grant, by no means disconcerted. "Tom Calder is from the same town as myself, and I wish him well."

Tom looked pleased at this friendly declaration on the part of Grant, whom, indeed, he personally liked better than Willis Ford, who evidently looked down upon him, and had more than once snubbed him.

"You see," said Ford, adroitly, "that Grant Thornton's old friend testifies against him. I don't think I need say any more except to deny, in toto, the statement of that low telegraph boy."

"I'm no lower than you are," retorted Johnny, angrily.

"None of your impertinence, boy!" said Ford, loftily.

"I must say," interposed the housekeeper, "that this seems a very discreditable conspiracy against my stepson. I am sure, Mr. Reynolds, you won't allow his reputation to be injured by such a base attack."

"Mr. Ford," said the broker, "I have listened attentively to what you have said. I ought to say that a telegraph boy has as much right to be believed as yourself."

"Even when there are three against him?"

"The three are interested parties."

"I have no doubt he is also. I presume he has an understanding with Grant Thornton, who is a suspected thief."

"I deny that, Mr. Ford," exclaimed Grant, indignantly.

"You are certainly suspected of stealing my stepmother's bonds."

"And I have no doubt you took them," declared the housekeeper, venomously.

At this time the doorbell was heard to ring.

"Excuse me for a moment," said the broker. "I will be back directly."

When he had left the room, the parties left behind looked at each other uncomfortably. Willis Ford, however, was too angry to keep silence.

He turned to Grant, and made an attack upon him.

"You won't accomplish anything, you young rascal, by your plotting and contriving! I give you credit for a good deal of cunning in bringing this boy to give the testimony he has; but it won't do you any good. Mr. Reynolds isn't a fool, and he will see through your design."

"That he will, Willis," said the housekeeper. "After all the kindness that boy has received in this house, he might be better employed than in stealing my bonds, and then trying to throw it upon a man like you."

"I don't care to argue with you, Mr. Ford," said Grant,

quietly. "You know as well as I do that I didn't steal the bonds, and you know," he added, significantly, "who did."

"I have a great mind to break your head, you impudent boy!"

"That would be a very poor argument. The truth has already come out, and I am vindicated."

"I don't know whether you expect Mr. Reynolds to shield you or not, but, if my mother takes my advice, she will have you arrested, whatever happens."

"I intend to," said the housekeeper, nodding spitefully. "If you had returned the bonds, I did not mean to let the matter drop, but since you have tried to throw suspicion on my son, who has always been devoted to me, I mean to punish you as severely as the law allows."

"I think you will change your mind, Mrs. Estabrook, and let the thief go unpunished," said Grant, in no ways disturbed.

"Not unless you make a full confession; and even then I think you ought to suffer for your base wickedness."

"You are making a mistake, Mrs. Estabrook. I referred to the thief."

"That is yourself."

Grant shrugged his shoulders. He was spared the necessity of answering the attack, for just then the door opened, and Mr. Reynolds re-entered. He did not enter alone, however.

A small man of quiet manner, attired in a sober suit of brown, closely followed him.

All present looked at him in surprise. Who was this man, and what had he to do with the matter that concerned them all?

They were not destined to remain long in doubt,

"Mr. Graham, gentlemen!" said the broker, with a wave of the hand.

The detective bowed courteously.

"Mr. Graham, permit me to ask," continued the broker, "if you have seen any of these gentlemen before?"

"Yes," answered Graham, and he indicated Grant Thornton, Jim Morrison and Tom Calder.

"When did you see them, and where?"

"At the Fifth Avenue Hotel this morning."

"What passed between them?"

"They were talking about some bonds, which that gentleman," indicating Morrison, "acknowledged giving to the boy to sell. He asked for the proceeds, but the boy told him there was something wrong about the bonds, and his employer wouldn't allow him to pass over the money. Upon this, Morrison, as I understand him to be called, said they were given him by a party that owed him money, and threatened that, if he had played a trick upon him, it would be the worse for him."

"Who is that man, Mr. Reynolds?" asked Ford, in nervous excitement.

"One of the best known detectives in the city," quietly answered the broker. "What have you to say to his evidence?"

"That it doesn't concern me. I may be wrong about the boy taking the bonds, but that doesn't involve me. There may have been another party."

"You forget the testimony of the telegraph boy - that he saw you give the bonds to your friend there."

"The boy told a falsehood!"

"I am in a position to confirm the boy's testimony," said the detective.

Willis Ford gasped for breath and seemed ready to sink into the floor. What was coming next?

CHAPTER XXIII

JUSTICE TRIUMPHS

Mr. Graham turned to the broker and addressed further remarks to him.

"Your statement that four hundred dollars remained to be accounted for, led me to conclude that they would be found in the possession of the party who had abstracted the others. I therefore obtained a search warrant and visited the room occupied by that gentleman, whose name I believe is Willis Ford."

This was an unexpected stroke. Ford did not speak, but kept his eyes fixed upon the detective in evident panic.

"I have just come from Mr. Ford's room," he resumed. "These are what I found there."

He drew from his pocket a long envelope, from which he took four government bonds.

"Will you be kind enough, Mrs. Estabrook," said the broker, gravely, "to examine these bonds and determine whether they are yours?"

The housekeeper took them mechanically and examined them.

"They are mine," she said; "but I cannot believe Willis took them."

"I did not," said Ford, hoarsely, but his eyes were downcast.

"Will you account for their being in your room, then, Mr. Ford?" inquired the broker, sternly.

"That boy must have put them there. I know nothing of them. I am as much surprised as you are."

"We have had enough of this, Mr. Ford," said the broker, coldly. "Your guilt is evident. In robbing your stepmother you have committed a serious crime; but in attempting to throw the guilt upon an innocent boy, you have been guilty of an offense still more detestable, and one which I cannot forgive. You cannot remain in my employment another day. If you will call at the office in the morning, I will pay your salary to the end of the month. That will end all relations between us."

Willis Ford looked like a convicted criminal. For the moment all his hardihood and bravado deserted him.

"Can this be true, Willis?" wailed his stepmother. "Is it possible that you took my bonds, and would have left me to an old age of poverty?"

"No," answered Ford, with a return of his usual assurance. "I am as innocent as a babe unborn. I am the victim of a conspiracy. As Mr. Reynolds is determined to shield his favorite by throwing the blame on it, I must submit. The time will come when he will acknowledge my innocence. Mother, I will satisfy you later, but I do not believe you will think me guilty. Gentlemen, I bid you all good-evening."

No one spoke as he withdrew from the room, and not even Morrison offered to follow him.

When he was fairly out of the room, the broker turned to Morrison.

"Mr. Morrison," he said, "I have a question or two to put to you. I think you will find it to your interest to answer correctly. Do you still maintain that these bonds were given you by Grant Thornton?"

"I may as well make a clean breast of it," said Morrison. "They were given me by Willis Ford."

"To satisfy a gambling debt, was it not?"

"Yes, sir."

"I take it for granted you did not know they were stolen?"

"If I had known it I wouldn't have touched them. I might have been suspected of stealing them myself."

"I believe you."

"You're a gentleman," said Morrison, gratified that his word was accepted.

"Of course you have lost the amount which you consider due you. To be entirely candid with you, I do not feel any sympathy with you. Money won at play must be classed among ill-gotten gains. I hope you will realize this, and give up a discreditable profession."

"I have no doubt your advice is good, sir. Do you want me and Tom any longer?"

"You are at liberty to go. I am indebted to you for coming. You have helped to clear up the mystery of the theft."

"He's a little hard on us, Tom," said Morrison, as they went down the front steps, "but he's treated us like a gentleman. That Ford is a rascal."

"I think so, too," Tom assented.

"And I shall never see a cent of that six hundred dollars," continued Jim Morrison, ruefully.

"If you'll excuse me, I'll go to my own room," said Mrs. Estabrook, pertly. "I want to think quietly of all this."

"Go, by all means," said the broker, courteously. "To-morrow morning your property shall be restored to you."

Next the detective and the telegraph boy withdrew, the latter rich by a five-dollar note, which Mr. Reynolds presented him.

Johnny's eyes sparkled.

"That will make mother happy," he said. "She'll think I am in luck."

"Keep your eyes open, my boy, and be faithful to your

employer, and this won't be the last piece of luck that will come your way."

When they were alone Mr. Reynolds turned to Grant and said kindly, "I congratulate you, Grant, on your complete vindication. Those who have wickedly conspired against you have come to grief, and you come out of the trial unscathed. As I am to part with Willis Ford, though you are not competent to take his place, your duties will be somewhat enlarged, and I will take care that your compensation shall be increased."

"I am afraid, Mr. Reynolds, I already receive more than I earn."

"That may be, but I am only anticipating a little. How much do I pay you now?"

"Six dollars a week, sir."

"I will allow you four dollars more, but this additional sum I will keep in my own hands, and credit you with. It is time you were saving something for future use. Will this be satisfactory to you?"

"You are very kind, Mr. Reynolds," said Grant. "I don't know how to thank you."

"Then I will tell you - be faithful in your duties in the office and continue your kindness to Herbert."

"Gladly, sir."

Grant decided not to write to his mother about his increase in salary. He preferred to wait till his savings amounted to a considerable sum, and then surprise her by the announcement of his good fortune. In six months, he estimated, he would have more than a hundred dollars, and this to the country minister's son seemed a large sum. At any rate, when he was twenty-one he might hope to be the possessor of a thousand dollars. This opened to Grant a brilliant prospect. It was probably all his father was worth, including all his possessions.

"In spite of my uncle's opposition," thought Grant, "I think I acted wisely in preferring business to college. Now I shall be able to make the family more comfortable."

When Willis Ford called at the office the next morning Grant was gone to the post office. As he returned he met Ford coming out with a check in his hand.

"So it's you, is it?" sneered Ford, stopping short.

"Yes, Mr. Ford."

"I suppose you are exulting over your victory?"

"You are mistaken," said Grant. "It was not my wish that anything unpleasant should happen."

"I suppose not," said Ford, in an unpleasant tone.

"For some reason you have shown a dislike to me from the first," Grant proceeded. "I don't know why. I have always treated you with respect and tried to do my duty faithfully."

"You are a little angel, to be sure."

"Have you any objection to telling me why you dislike me?" he asked.

"Yes, I'll tell you. It is because I see how you are trying to worm yourself into the confidence of Mr. Reynolds. You have plotted against me, and now, thanks to you, I have lost my place."

"I don't consider myself the cause of that, Mr. Ford."

"I do. But you needn't exult too much. I generally pay my debts, and I shan't forget what I owe you. I will be even with you some day."

So saying, he walked off, and Grant returned to his work.

"I can't understand why Mr. Ford should hate me so," he thought.

CHAPTER XXIV

STARTLING NEWS

Willis Ford's feelings were far from enviable when he took leave of the office in which he had long enjoyed an excellent position. He was conscious, though scarcely willing to admit it, that his misfortunes had been brought upon him by his own unwise, not to say criminal, course. None the less, however, was he angry with those whom he had connected with the disaster that had come upon him. He had always disliked Grant Thornton. Now he hated him, and thirsted for an opportunity to do him mischief. Next he felt embittered against Mr. Reynolds, who had discharged him, though it is hardly possible to see how the broker could have done otherwise. This dislike was increased within a few days, and for this reason.

Ford addressed a letter to Mr. Reynolds, requesting a certificate of good character, which would enable him to procure a new situation.

To this request the broker answered substantially as follows:

"I shall be glad to hear that you have changed your course, and have decided to lead an honest lift; but, for the same reason that I am not willing to retain you in my employment, I am unwilling to recommend you without reserve to another business man. If you are willing to refer him to me, on condition that I tell the truth, I will cheerfully testify that you have discharged your office duties to my satisfaction."

"The old fool!" muttered Ford, angrily crushing the letter in his hand. "What use would such a recommendation be to me? Not content with discharging me, he wants to keep me out of employment."

In truth, Willis Ford hardly knew where to turn. He had saved no money, and was earning nothing. In his dilemma he turned to his stepmother.

One forenoon, after he knew the broker and Grant would be out of the way, he rang the bell, and inquired for the housekeeper.

Mrs. Estabrook was agitated when she saw her stepson. She did not like to believe that he had robbed her, but it was hard to believe otherwise.

"Oh, Willis!" she said almost bursting into tears, "how could you take my small savings? I would not have believed you capable of it!"

"You don't mean to say, mother," returned Willis, with well-dissembled and reproachful sorrow, "that you believe this monstrous slander?"

"I don't want to believe it, Willis, heaven knows. But were not the bonds found in your room?"

"I admit it," said Ford; "but how did they get there?"

"Did you not put them there?"

"Certainly not, mother. I thought you knew me better than that."

"But who, then -" began his step-mother, looking bewildered.

"Who should it be but that boy?"

"Grant Thornton?"

"Yes."

"Have you any proof of this?" asked the housekeeper, eagerly.

"I will tell you what I have found out. I learn that a boy called, on the day in question, at my room and asked to see me. Being told that I was out, he asked leave to go up and wait for me. As the servant had no suspicion, he was allowed to go up. I don't know how long he stayed; but no doubt he had the bonds with him and concealed them where they were found."

"Did you ask for a description of the boy? Was it like Grant?" asked the housekeeper, quickly.

"Unfortunately, the girl did not take particular notice of him. I have no doubt that it was either Grant or the telegraph boy, who seems to have been in the plot."'

Now, this story was an audacious fiction, and should not have imposed upon a person of ordinary intelligence; but the housekeeper was anxious to believe her step-son innocent and Grant guilty. She therefore accepted it without question, and was loud in her denunciation of that "artful young rascal."

"You ought to tell Mr. Reynolds of this, Willis," she said.

"It would be of no use, mother. He is too strongly prejudiced against me. What do you think? He has refused me a letter of recommendation. What does he care if I starve?" concluded Willis, bitterly.

"But I care, Willis. I will not desert you," said Mrs. Estabrook, in a tone of sympathy.

This was just the mood in which Ford desired his step-mother to be. He was desirous of effecting a loan, and after a time succeeded in having transferred to him two of the one-hundred-dollar bonds. He tried hard to obtain the five hundred, but Mrs. Estabrook was too prudent and too much attached to her savings to consent to this. Ford had to be satisfied with considerably less.

"Ought I to stay with Mr. Reynolds after he has treated you in this way, Willis?" asked his step-mother, anxiously.

"By all means, mother. You don't want to throw away a good position."

"But it will be hard to see that boy high in Mr. Reynolds' confidence, after all his wickedness."

"You must dissemble, mother. Treat him fairly, and watch your opportunity to harm him and serve me. Don't say much about me, for it would do no good; but keep your hold on Reynolds."

"If you think it best, Willis," said his stepmother, not without a feeling of relief, for she was reluctant to relinquish a good home and liberal salary, "I will remain."

"Do so by all means. We may as well make all we can out of the enemy, for Mr. Reynolds has treated me very shabbily. And now I must bid you good-by."

"What are your plans, Willis?"

"I can't tell you, but I think I shall go West."

"And I shall never see you!"

"You will hear from me, and I hope I shall have good news to write."

Willis Ford left the house, and, going to the Grand Central Depot, bought a ticket for Chicago.

Now came quite a pleasant period after the trouble and excitement. Grant found his duties at the office increased, and it was pleasant to see that his employer reposed confidence in him. His relations with others in the office were pleasant, now that Willis Ford was away, and every day he seemed to get new insight into the details of the business. Whether Jim Morrison and Tom Calder were in the city, he did not know. At all events, they were never seen in the neighborhood of Wall Street. Grant was not sorry to have them pass out of his life, for he did not consider that he was likely to draw any benefit from their presence and companionship.

He was still a member of Mr. Reynolds' house-hold. Herbert appeared to be as much attached to him as if he were an older brother, and the broker looked with pleasure upon the new happiness that beamed from the face of his son.

As to Mrs. Estabrook, Grant had feared that she would continue to show animosity toward him, but he had nothing to complain of. She certainly did not show any cordiality in her necessary intercourse with him; but then, on the other hand, she did not manifest any desire to injure him. This was all Grant desired. He felt that under no circumstances could he have made a friend of the housekeeper. He was content to have her leave him alone.

After the lapse of six months Grant expressed a desire to go home to pass a day or two. His mother's birthday was close at hand, and he had bought for her a present which he knew would be acceptable. Permission was readily accorded, and Grant passed four happy days at home. His parents were pleased that he was so highly regarded by his employer, and had come to think that Grant's choice had been a wise one.

When Grant returned he went at once to the office. He found it a scene of excitement.

"What has happened?" he asked, eagerly.

"Herbert Reynolds has disappeared, and his father is almost beside himself with grief!" was the startling reply.

CHAPTER XXV.

ANXIOUS INQUIRIES

After a while Grant learned the particulars about Herbert's disappearance. He had gone out to play in the street about three o'clock in the afternoon. Generally he waited for Grant to return-home, but during his absence he had found other companions. When his father returned home, he inquired of the housekeeper: "Where is Herbert?"

"He went out to play," said Mrs. Estabrook, indifferently.

"In the street?"

"I believe so."

"He ought to be in by this time."

"Probably he went to walk with some of his companions. As he had no watch, he might not know that it is so late."

This seemed very plausible to Mr. Reynolds.

"Yes," he said; "Herbert seems lost without Grant. He will be glad to see him back."

To this Mrs. Estabrook did not reply. She had learned, to her cost, that it would not be politic to speak against Grant, and she was not disposed to praise him. She seldom mentioned him at all.

The dinner bell rang, and still Herbert had not returned. His father began to feel anxious.

"It is strange that Herbert remains so long away," he said.

"I shouldn't wonder if he had gone to Central Park on some excursion," returned the housekeeper calmly.

"You think there is nothing wrong?" asked the broker, anxiously.

"How could there be here, sir?" answered Mrs. Estabrook, with unruffled demeanor.

This answer helped to calm Mr. Reynolds, who ordered dinner delayed half an hour.

When, however, an hour - two hours - passed, and the little boy still remained absent, the father's anxiety became insupportable. He merely tasted a few spoonfuls of soup, and found it impossible to eat more. The housekeeper, on the contrary, seemed quite unconcerned, and showed her usual appetite.

"I am seriously anxious, Mrs. Estabrook," said the broker. "I will take my hat and go out to see if I can gain any information. Should Herbert return while I am away, give him his supper, and, if he is tired, let him go to bed, just finding out why he was out so late."

"Very well, sir."

When Mr. Reynolds had left the house a singular expression of gratified malice swept over the housekeeper's face. "It is just retribution," she murmured. "He condemned and discharged my stepson for the sin of another. Now it is his own heart that bleeds."

Only a few steps from his own door the broker met a boy about two years older than Herbert, with whom the latter sometimes played.

"Harvey," he said, "have you seen Herbert this afternoon?"

"Yes, sir; I saw him about three o'clock."

"Where?" asked the broker, anxiously.

"Just 'round the corner of the block," answered Harvey Morrison.

"Was he alone?"

"No; there was a young man with him - about twenty, I should think."

"A young man! Was it one you had ever saw before?"

"No, sir."

"What was his appearance?"

Harvey described Herbert's companion as well as he could, but the anxious father did not recognize the description.

"Did you speak to Herbert? Did you ask where he was going?"

"Yes, sir. He told me that you had sent for him to go on an excursion."

"Did he say that?" asked the father, startled.

"Yes, sir."

"Then there is some mischief afoot. I never sent for him," said the agitated father.

Mr. Reynolds requested Harvey to accompany him to the nearest police station, and relate all that he knew to the officer in charge, that the police might be put on the track. He asked himself in vain what object any one could have in spiriting away the boy, but no probable explanation occurred to him.

On his return to the house he communicated to the housekeeper what he had learned.

"What do you think of it?" he asked.

"It may be only a practical joke," answered the housekeeper calmly.

"Heaven grant it may be nothing more! But I fear it is something far more serious."

"I dare say it's only a boy's lark, Mr. Reynolds."

"But you forget - it was a young man who was seen in

his company."

"I really don't know what to think of it, then. I don't believe the boy will come to any harm."

Little sleep visited the broker's pillow that night, but the housekeeper looked fresh and cheerful in the morning.

"Has the woman no feeling?" thought the anxious father, as he watched the tranquil countenance of the woman who for five years had been in charge of his house.

When she was left alone in the house Mrs. Estabrook took from her workbasket a letter, bearing date a month previous, and read slowly the following paragraph: "I have never forgotten the wrong done me by Mr. Reynolds. He discharged me summarily from his employment and declined to give me a recommendation which would secure me a place elsewhere. I swore at the time that I would get even with him, and I have never changed my resolution. I shall not tell you what I propose to do. It is better that you should not know. But some day you will hear something that will surprise you. When that time comes, if you suspect anything, say nothing. Let matters take their course."

The letter was signed by Willis Ford.

CHAPTER XXVI.

A WESTERN CABIN

"Abner!"

The speaker was a tall, gaunt woman, in a loose, faded, calico dress, and she stood at the door of a cabin in a Western clearing.

"What yer want?" came as a reply from a tall, unhealthy-looking boy in overalls, who was sitting on a log in the yard.

"I want you to split some wood for the stove."

"I'm tired," drawled the boy.

"I'll tire you!" said the mother, sharply. "You tall, lazy, good-for-nothing drone! Here I've been up since five o'clock, slavin' for you and your drunken father. Where's he gone?"

"To the village, I reckon."

"To the tavern, I reckon. It's there that he spends all the money he gets hold of; he never gives me a cent. This is the only gown I've got, except an old alpaca. Much he cares!"

"It isn't my fault, is it?" asked the boy, indifferently.

"You're a-follerin' in his steps. You'll be just another Joel Barton - just as shif'less and lazy. Just split me some wood before I get hold of yer!"

Abner rose slowly, went to the shed for an ax, and in the most deliberate manner possible began to obey his mother's commands.

The cabin occupied by Abner and his parents was far from being a palace. It contained four rooms, but the furniture was of the most primitive description. Joel Barton, the nominal head of the famliy, was the possessor of eighty acres of land, from which he might have obtained a comfortable living, for the soil was productive; but he was lazy, shiftless and intemperate, as his wife had described him. Had he been as active and energetic as she was, he might have been in very different circumstances. It is no wonder that the poor woman was fretted and irritated almost beyond endurance, seeing how all her industry was neutralized by her husband's habits. Abner took after his father, though he had not yet developed a taste for drink, and was perfectly contented with their poor way of living, as long as he was not compelled to work hard. What little was required of him he would shirk if he possibly could.

This cabin was situated about a mile from the little village which had gathered round the depot. The name of the township was Scipio, though it is doubtful if one in fifty of the inhabitants knew after whom it was named. In fact, the name was given by a schoolmaster, who had acquired some rudiments of classical learning at a country academy.

To the depot we must transport the reader, on the arrival of the morning train from Chicago. But two passengers got out. One of them was a young man under twenty. The other was a boy, apparently about ten years of age, whom he held firmly by the hand.

He was a delicate-looking boy, and, though he was dressed in a coarse, ill-fitting suit, he had an appearance of refinement and gentle nature, as if he had been brought up in a luxurious home. He looked sad and anxious, and the glances he fixed on his companion indicated that he held him in fear.

"Where are you going?" he asked timidly, looking about him apprehensively.

"You'll know soon enough," was the rough reply.

"When are you going to take me home, Mr. Ford?" asked the boy, in a pleading tone.

"Don't trouble yourself about that."

"Papa will be so anxious about me - papa and Grant!"

The young man's brow contracted.

"Don't mention the name of that boy! I hate him."

"He was always good to me. I liked so much to be with him."

"He did all he could to injure me. I swore to be even with him, and I will!"

"But I have never injured you, Mr. Ford."

"How could you - a baby like you?" said Ford, contemptuously.

"Then why did you take me from home, and make me so unhappy?"

"Because it was the only way in which I could strike a blow at your father and Grant Thornton. When your father dismissed me, without a recommendation, not caring whether I starved or not, he made me his enemy."

"But he wouldn't if you hadn't - "

"Hadn't what?" demanded Ford, sternly.

"Taken Mrs. Estabrook's bonds."

"Dare to say that again, and I will beat you," said Willis Ford, brutally.

Herbert trembled, for he had a timid nature, and an exquisite susceptibility to pain.

"I didn't mean to offend you," he said.

"You'd better not. Wait here a minutes, while I look around for some one of whom I can make inquiries. Here, sit dowp on that settee, and, mind you, don't stir till I come back. Will you obey me?"

"Yes," answered the boy, submissively.

CHAPTER XXVII

THE RIDE TO BARTON'S

Willis Ford went to the station master, who stood at the door with a cheap cigar in his mouth.

"Is there a man named Joel Barton living hereabouts?" he asked.

The station master took his cigar from his mouth and surveyed his questioner with some curiosity.

"Does he owe you money?" he inquired.

"No," answered Ford, impatiently. "Will you answer my question?"

"You needn't be in such a pesky hurry," drawled the station master. "Yes, he lives up the road a piece."

"How far is a piece?"

"Well, maybe a mile."

"Straighten?"

"Yes."

"Is there any way of riding?"

"Well, stranger, I've got a team myself. Is that boy with you?"

"Yes."

"I'll take you over for half a dollar."

"Can you go at once?"

"Yes."

"Then it's a bargain."

The station master, whose house was only three minutes' walk away, appeared in a reasonable time with a farm wagon, drawn by an old horse that had seen better days, it is to be hoped, for she was a miserable-looking mare.

"Jump in, Herbert," said Ford.

The boy obeyed, and sat on the front seat, between the driver and his abductor.

"I suppose the horse is warranted not to run away?" said Ford, regarding the animal with a smile.

"He ran away with me once," was the unexpected answer.

"When was that?"

"'Bout fifteen years ago," replied the driver, with grim humor. "I reckon he's steadied down by this time."

"It looks like it," said Ford.

"Know Joel Barton?" asked the station master, after a pause.

"I saw him once when I was a boy."

"Any relation?"

"He married a cousin of my stepmother. What sort of a man is he?"

"He's a no-account man - shif'less, lazy - drinks."

"That agrees with what I have heard. How about his wife?"

"She's smart enough. If he was like her they'd live comfortably. She has a hard time with him and Abner - Abner's her son, and just like his father, only doesn't drink yet. Like as not he will when he gets older."

Willis Ford was not the only listener to this colloquy. Herbert paid attention to every word, and in the poor boy's mind there was the uncomfortable query, "Why are we going to these people?" He would know soon, probably, but he had a presentiment of trouble.

"Yes," continued the station master, "Mrs. Barton has a hard row to hoe; but she's a match for Joel."

"What do you mean by that?"

"She's got a temper of her own, and she can talk a man deaf, dumb, and blind. She gives Barton a piece of her mind whenever he comes home full."

"She ought to have that satisfaction. From what you tell me, I don't feel very proud of my unknown relatives."

"Goin' to stay there any length of time?"

"I don't know my own plans yet," answered Willis Ford, with a glance at the boy. He foresaw a scene when he announced his purpose to leave Herbert in this unpromising place, but he did not wish to anticipate it.

"I suppose Barton is a farmer?" he suggested.

"He pretends to be, but his farm doesn't pay much."

"What supports them?"

"His wife takes in work from the tailors in the the village. Then they've got a cow, and she makes butter. As for Joel, he brings in precious little money. He might pick up a few dollars hirin' out by the day, if he wasn't so lazy. I had a job for him myself one day, but he knocked off at noon - said he was tuckered out, and wanted me to pay him for that half day. I knew well enough where the money would go, so I told him I wouldn't pay him unless he worked until sunset."

"Did he do it?"

"Yes, he did; but he grumbled a good deal. When he got his pay he went over to Thompson's saloon, and he didn't leave it until all the money was spent. When his wife heard of it she was mad, and I expect she gave Joel a taste of the broom handle."

"I wouldn't blame her much."

"Nor I. But here we are. Yonder's Barton's house. Will you get out?"

"Yes."

Abner, who was sitting on a stump, no sooner saw the team stop than he ran into the house, in some excitement, to tell the news.

"Marm," he said, "there's a team stopped, and there's a man and boy gettin' out; 'spect they're coming here."

"Lord's sake! Who be they?"

"Dunno."

"Well, go out and tell 'em I'll see' em in a minute."

Abner met them in front of the house.

"Are you Joel Barton's son?" asked Ford.

"That's what the old man says," returned Abner, with a grin.

"Is your mother at home?"

"Marm will be right out. She's slickin' up. Who be you?"

"You'll know in good time, my boy." "Who's he? Is he your son?"

"No," answered Herbert promptly.

Willis Ford turned upon his young ward with a frown.

He understood the boy's tone.

"It will be time to speak when you are spoken to," he said sharply.

"Here's marm'" said Abner, as his mother's tall figure appeared in the doorway.

CHAPTER XXVIII

HERBERT IS PROVIDED WITH A NEW HOME

Mrs. Barton regarded the newcomers with a wondering stare.

"Did you want to see Joel?" she asked.

"I shall be glad to see him in due time, Mrs. Barton," returned Willis Ford, with unwonted politeness; "but I came principally to see you."

"Who be you?" inquired Mrs. Barton, unceremoniously; "I don't know you no more'n the dead."

"There is a slight connection between us, however. I am the stepson of Pauline Estabrook, of New York, who is a cousin of yours."

"You don't say Pauline is your mother?" ejaculated the lady of the house. "Well, I never expected to see kith or kin of hers out here. Is that your son?"

"No, Mrs. Barton; but he is under my charge."

Herbert was about to disclaim this, but an ominous frown from Willis Ford intimidated him.

"My name is Willis Ford; his is Sam Green."

Herbert's eyes opened wide with astonishment at this statement.

"My name is -" he commenced.

"Silence!" hissed Ford, with a menacing look. "You must not contradict me."

"I s'pose I ought to invite you to stay here," said Mrs. Barton, awkwardly; "but he's so shif-less, and such a poor provider, that I ain't got anything in the house fit for dinner."

"Thank you," returned Ford, with an inward shudder. "I shall dine at the hotel; but I have a little business matter to speak of, Mrs. Barton, and I would wish to speak in private. I will come into the house, with your permission, and we will leave the two boys together."

"Come right in," said Mrs. Barton, whose curiosity was aroused. "Here, you Abner, just take care of the little boy."

Abner proceeded to do this, first thinking it necessary to ask a few questions.

"Where do you live when you're at home, Sam?" he asked.

"In New York; but my name isn't Sam," replied Herbert.

"What is it, then?"

"Herbert."

"What makes him call you Sam, then?" asked Abner, with a jerk of the finger toward the house.

"I don't know, except he is afraid I will be found."

Abner looked puzzled.

"Is he your guardeen?" he asked.

"No; he was my father's clerk."

"Ho! Did your father have clerks?"

"Yes; he is a rich man and does business in New York."

"What made him send you out here?"

"He didn't."

"Then why did you come?"

"Mr. Ford was mad with papa, and stole me away."

"He wouldn't steal me away easy!" said Abner, defiantly; "but, then, I ain't a little kid like you."

"I'm not a kid," said Herbert, who was not used to slang.

"Oh, you don't know what I mean - you're a little boy and couldn't do nothin'. If he tried to take me, he'd find his hands full."

Herbert, who was not very much prepossessed by Abner's appearance, thought it very doubtful whether any one would ever attempt to kidnap him.

"What's he goin' to do with you?" continued Abner.

"I don't know. I expect he'll make papa pay a good sum to get me back."

"Humph!" remarked Abner, surveying with some contempt the small proportions of the boy before him. "You ain't much good. I don't believe he'll pay much for you."

Tears sprang to the eyes of the little boy, but he forced them back.

"My papa would think differently," he said.

"Papa!" mimicked Abner. "Oh, how nice we are! Why don't you say dad, like I do?"

"Because it isn't a nice name. Papa wouldn't like to have me call him so."

"Where did you get them clothes? I don't think much of 'em."

"Nor I," answered Herbert. "They're not my own clothes. Mr. Ford bought them for me in Chicago."

"He must like you, to buy you new clothes."

"No, he doesn't. My own clothes were much nicer. He sold them. He was afraid some one would know me in the others."

"I wonder what he and marm are talking about so long?"

This question Herbert was unable to answer. He did not guess how nearly this conversation affected him.

No sooner had the two entered the house than Willis Ford began.

"Mrs. Barton," he said, "I'll tell you now what brought me here."

"Go ahead," said the lady, encouragingly.

"I want you to take the boy I have brought with me to board."

"Land sakes! I don't keep a boardin' house!"

"No; but if I will make it worth your while you will take him, won't you?"

"How much will you give?" asked Mrs. Barton, shrewdly.

"Four dollars a week."

"He'll be a sight of trouble," said the lady; but there was something in her tone that satisfied Ford that she was favorably inclined to the proposal.

"Oh, no, he won't. He's so small that you can twist him round your finger. Besides, Abner will be company for him. He will be with him most of the time."

"Say five dollars and it's a bargain," said Mrs. Barton.

Ford hesitated. He did not care to spend more than he was obliged to, but it was of importance to obtain at least a temporary refuge for the boy, of whose care he was heartily tired. It seemed to him that five dollars would be enough to support the whole family in the style in which they were apparently accustomed to live. However, it was politic to make the sum sufficient to interest these people in retaining charge of the boy.

"Well," he said, after a pause, "it's more than I expected to pay, but I suppose I shall have to accept your terms. I conclude Mr. Barton will not object to your taking a boarder?"

"Oh, Joel is of no account," returned Mrs. Barton, contemptuously. "I run this house!"

Willis Ford suppressed a smile. He could easily believe from Mrs. Barton's appearance that she was the head of the establishment.

"There's one thing more," added Mrs. Barton; "you're to pay the money to me. Jest as sure as it goes into Joel's hands, it'll go for drink. The way that man carries on is a disgrace."

"I should prefer to pay the money to you," said Ford.

"You'll have to pay somethin' in advance, if you want the boy to have anythin' to eat. I've got to send to the village, and I haven't got a cent in the house."

Willis Ford took out a pocketbook. Extracting therefrom four five-dollar bills, he handed them to Mrs. Barton.

"There's money for four weeks," he said. "When that time is up I'll send you more."

Mrs. Barton's eyes sparkled, and she eagerly clutched the money.

"I ain't seen so much money for years," she said. "I'll jest look out Joel don't get hold of it. Don't you tell Joel or Abner how much you've paid me."

"I'll take care of that, Mrs. Barton. By the way, I must caution you not to believe any of the boy's stories. He's the son of a friend of mine, who's put him under my care. The boy's weak-minded, and has strange fancies. He thinks his name isn't Sam Green, and that his father is rich. Why, only the other day he insisted his name was George Washington."

"Land's sake! How cur'us!" "Of course; you won't pay any attention to what he says. He may take it into his head to run away. If he does, you must get him back."

"You can trust me to do that!" said Mrs. Barton, with emphasis. "I ain't goin' to let no five-dollar boarder slip through my fingers!"

"That's well! Now I must be going. You will hear from me from time to time."

He passed through the front door into the yard.

"Good-by!" he said.

Herbert was about to follow him, but he waived him back.

"You are not to come with me, Sam," he said. "I shall leave you for a few weeks with this good lady."

Herbert stared at him in dismay. This was something he had never dreamed of.

CHAPTER XXIX

INTRODUCES MR. BARTON

When Herbert realized that he was to be left behind he ran after Willis Ford, and pleaded for the privilege of accompanying him. "Don't leave me here, Mr. Ford!" he said. "I should die of homesickness!"

"So you would rather go with me?" Ford said, with an amused smile.

"Oh, yes, much rather!"

"I had not supposed you valued my company so highly. I ought to feel complimented. I am sorry to disappoint you, but I shall have to leave you here for a few weeks. This good lady will take good care of you."

Herbert stole a glance at Mrs. Barton, who was watching him with mingled contempt and impatience, but he did not become any more reconciled to the prospect. He reiterated his request.

"I have had enough of this," said Ford, sternly. "You will stop making a fuss if you know what is best for yourself. Good-by! You will hear from me soon."

Herbert realized the uselessness of his resistance, and

sank despondently upon the grass.

"Is he goin' to stay here, marm?" asked Abner, curiously.

"Yes; he's goin' to board with us."

"Ho, ho!" laughed Abner; "he'll have a nice boardin' place!"

"Abner, you jest shut up, or I'll take a stick to you! You needn't make him any more homesick than he is. Just try ef you can't amuse him."

"Say, Sam, I guess we'll have a stavin' time together," said Abner, really pleased to have a companion. "What'll we do? Want to play leapfrog?"

"I don't feel like playing," answered Herbert, despondently.

"We might go fishin'," suggested Abner. "There's a pond only a quarter of a mile from here."

"I don't know how to fish," said Herbert.

"Don't know how to fish? What do you know how to do?"

"We don't have any chance in New York."

"Say," exclaimed Abner, with sudden interest, "is New York a nice place?"

"I wish I was back there. I never shall be happy anywhere's else."

"Tell me what you fellows do there. I dunno but I'd like to go myself."

Before Herbert had a chance to answer Mrs. Barton broke in:

"Abner, you take care of Sam while I go to the village."

"What are you goin' there for, marm?"

"I'm going to buy some sausages for dinner. We haven't got anything in the house."

"Me and Sam will go, if you'll give us the money."

"I know you too well, Abner Barton. I won't trust you with the money. Ef I gave you a five-dollar bill, I'd never see any on't back again."

"Say, mam, you haven't got a five-dollar bill, have you?" asked Abner, with distended eyes.

"Never you mind!"

"I'll tell dad ef you don't give me some."

"You jest dare to do it!" returned Mrs. Barton, in a menacing tone. "Your father ain't got nothin' to do with it. It's money for Sam's board."

"My name isn't Sam," expostulated Herbert, who had a natural preference for his own appellation.

"That's what I'm goin' to call you. You can call yourself George Washington, or General Jackson, ef you want to. Mebbe you're Christopher Columbus."

"My name is Herbert Reynolds," said Herbert, annoyed.

"That's what you call yourself to-day. There's no knowin' who you'll be to-morrow."

"Don't you believe me, Mrs. Barton?" asked Herbert, distressed.

"No, I don't. The man who brung you - I dis-remember his name -"

"Willis Ford."

"Well, Willis Ford, then! It seems you know his name. Well, he told me you was loony, and thought you was somebody else than your own self."

"He told you that I was crazy?" ejaculated Herbert.

"Yes; and I have no doubt it's so."

"It's a wicked lie!" exclaimed Herbert, indignantly; "and I'd like to tell him so to his face."

"Well, you won't have a chance for some time. But I can't stand here talkin'. I must be goin' to the store. You two behave yourselves while I'm gone!"

Herbert felt so dull and dispirited that he did not care to speak, but Abner's curiosity had been excited about New York, and he plied his young companion with questions, which Herbert answered wearily. Though he responded listlessly, and did not say any more than he felt obliged to, he excited Abner's interest.

"I mean to go to New York some time," he said. "Is it far?"

"It's as much as a thousand miles. It may be more."

"Phew! That's a big distance. How did you come?"

"We came in the cars."

"Did it cost much?"

"I don't know. Mr. Ford paid for the tickets."

"Has he got plenty of money?"

"I don't think he has. He used to be pa's clerk."

"I wish we had enough money. You and me would start some fine mornin', and mebbe your father would give me something to do when we got there."

For the first time Herbert began to feel an interest in the conversation.

"Oh, I wish we could," he said, fervently. "I know pa would give you a lot of money for bringing me back."

"Do you really think he would?" asked Abner, briskly.

"I know he would. But your mother wouldn't let us go."

"She wouldn't know it," said Abner, winking.

"You wouldn't run away from home?" questioned Herbert.

"Why wouldn't I? What's to keep me here? Marm's always scoldin', and dad gets drunk whenever he has any money to spend for drink. I reckon they wouldn't care much if I made myself scarce."

Herbert was not sure whether he ought not to feel shocked. He admitted to himself, however, that if he had a father and mother answering the description of Abner's, that he would not so much regret leaving them. At any rate, Abner's words awoke a hope of sometime getting away from the place he already hated, and returning to his city home, now more valued than ever.

"We can't go without money," he said, in a troubled voice.

"Couldn't we walk?"

"It's too far, and I'm not strong."

"I could walk it, ef I took time enough," asserted Abner, positively. "Hello! there's dad!"

Herbert looked up, and, following Abner's glance, saw a man approaching the farmhouse. Mr. Barton - for it was he - was a tall man, shabbily attired, his head crowned with a battered hat, whose gait indicated a little uncertainty, and betrayed some difficulty about the maintenance of his equilibrium.

"Is that your father?" asked Herbert.

"It's the old man, sure enough. He's about half full."

"What's that?"

"He's been drinkin', as usual; but he didn't drink enough to make him tight. Guess his funds give out."

Herbert was rather shocked at Abner's want of respect in speaking of his father, but even to him Mr. Barton hardly seemed like a man who could command a son's respect.

"Wonder whether dad met marm on the way?" said Abner, musing.

By this time, Mr. Barton had entered the yard, and caught sight of his son and Herbert.

"Abner," said he, in a thick voice, "who's that boy?"

"Then he didn't meet marm," thought Abner. "He's a boy that's goin' to board with us, dad," he answered.

"You don't say! Glad to make your acquaintance, boy," he said, straightening up.

"Thank you, sir," answered Herbert, faintly.

CHAPTER XXX

A MODEL HOUSEHOLD

"When did you come?" asked Barton, steadying himself against a tree.

"Half an hour ago," answered Abner, for Herbert was gazing, with a repulsion he found it difficult to conceal, at Barton, whose flushed face and thick utterance indicated his condition very clearly.

"Who came with him?" continued Barton.

"You'd better ask marm. She attended to the business. It was a young man."

"Where is she?"

"Gone to the village to buy some sassiges for dinner."

"Good!" exclaimed Barton, in a tone of satisfaction. "I'll stay at home to dinner to-day. Did the man pay your mother any money?"

"I s'pose so, or she wouldn't be buyin' sassiges. Old Schickman won't trust us any more."

"The money should have been paid to me. I'll see about

it when your marm comes back from the store."

"You'd spend it all for drink, dad," said Abner.

"How dare you speak so to your father, you ungrateful young dog!"

He essayed to reach Abner to strike him, but his dutiful son dodged easily, and his father, being unsteady on his legs, fell on the ground.

Abner laughed, but Herbert was too much shocked to share in his enjoyment.

"Come here and help me up, you Abner!" said his father.

"Not much, dad! If you hadn't tried to lick me you wouldn't have fallen!"

"Let me help you, sir!" said Herbert, conquering his instinctive disgust and approaching the fallen man.

"You're a gentleman!" murmured Barton, as he took the little boy's proffered hand and, after considerable ado, raised himself to a standing position. "You're a gentleman; I wish I had a boy like you."

Herbert could not join in the wish. He felt that a father like Joel Barton would be a great misfortune.

But just then Mrs. Barton entered the yard, marching with long strides like a man's.

"Here's marm!" announced Abner.

Barton steadied himself as he turned to look at his wife.

"I want to see you, Mrs. B.," he said. "When are you goin' to have dinner?"

"Never, if I depended on you to supply the vittles!" she answered, bluntly.

"Don't speak so before a stranger," said Barton, with a hiccough. "You hurt my feelin's."

"Your feelin's are tough, and so are mine by this time."

"What have you got there?"

"Some sassiges. Ef you want your share, you'll have to be on time. I shan't save you any."

"How much money did the man pay you, Mrs. B.?"

"That's my business!" retorted his wife, shortly.

"Mrs. B.," said her husband, straightening up, "I want you to understand that I'm the master of this house, and it's my right to take care of the money. You'll oblige me by handin' it over."

"I'll do nothing of the sort, Joel Barton! You'd only spend it for drink."

"Would you grudge me the few pennies I spend for drink? My system requires it. That's what the doctor says."

"Then you must find the money for it yourself. My

system requires something to eat, and, ef I take a boarder, he's got to have something to eat, too."

"Mrs. B., I didn't think your heart was so hard," said Barton, in a maudlin tone.

"Look here, Joel Barton; you might as well stop such foolish talk. It won't do no good. I can't stay here all day. I must go and be gettin' dinner."

Had Barton succeeded in raising money from his wife, he would probably have returned at once to the tavern, and his place would have been vacant at the dinner table. Failing in this, he lay back and fell asleep, and was not roused till dinner time.

Mrs. Barton was a fair cook, and Herbert ate with an unexpected relish. It is needless to say that Abner also did full justice to the meal.

"I say, Sam," he said, "I'm glad you've come."

Herbert was hardly prepared to agree with him.

"Now we'll have to live better," Abner explained. "Mam and I gen'ally have to skirmish round for vittles. We don't often get meat."

This frank confession rather alarmed Herbert. He was not over self-indulgent, but he had never lacked for nourishing food, and the prospect of an uncertain supply was not encouraging.

When dinner was over - there was no second course - they left the table. Joel Barton made a fresh attempt to extort a small sum from his wife, but was met with an inflexible refusal. Mrs. Barton proved deaf alike to entreaties and threats. She was a strong, resolute woman, and not one to be intimidated.

When Barton left the house, his look of disappointment had given place to one of cunning.

"Come here, Abner!" he said, beckoning to his son and heir.

"What for?"

"Never you mind."

"But I do mind. Do you want to catch hold of me?"

"No; it's only a little matter of business. It's for your good."

Abner accompanied his father as far as the fence.

"Now, what do you want?" he asked, with his eyes warily fixed on his father.

"I want you to find out where your marm keeps that money," said Barton, in a coaxing tone.

"What for?"

"You're to take it and bring it to me."

"And go without eatin'?"

"I'll buy the provisions myself. I'm the head of the family."

"Do you want me to hook money from marm?"

"'Twon't be hookin'. The money by right belongs to me. Ain't I the head of the family?"

"I dunno about that. Marm's the boss, and always has been," chuckled Abner.

Joel frowned, but immediately tried another attack.

"Of course I'll give you some of it, Abner," he resumed. "If there's five dollars I'll give you a quarter."

"I'll see about it, dad."

"Get it for me before evenin', if you can. I shall need it then."

Abner returned to Herbert, and frankly related the conversation that had taken place between himself and his father.

Herbert was shocked. He did not know what to think of the singular family he had got into.

"You won't do it, will you?" he asked, startled.

"No, I won't. I want a quarter bad enough, but I'd rather mam would keep the money. She'll spend it for vittles, and dad would spend it for drink. Wouldn't you like to go a-fishin'? It's fine weather, and we'll have fun."

Herbert assented, not knowing how to dispose of his time. Abner turned the conversation again on New York. What Herbert had already told him had powerfully impressed his imagination.

"Haven't you got any money?" he asked.

"No," answered Herbert. "Mr. Ford took away all I had, except this."

He drew from his pocket a nickel.

"That won't do no good," said Abner, disappointed. "Stop a minute, though," he added, after aminute's pause. "Wouldn't your folks send you some money, if you should write to them?"

"Yes," answered Herbert, his face brightening. "Why didn't I think of that before? If I could get me paper and ink I'd write at once to papa. I know he'd either send the money or come for me."

"We'll go to the post office," said Abner. "There you can buy some paper and a postage stamp. You've got just money enough. There's a pen and ink there."

"Let us go at once," said Herbert, eagerly.

The boys took their way to the village. The letter was written and posted, and a burden was lifted from the boy's mind. He felt that his father would seek him out at once, and he could bear his present position for a short time. But, alas! for poor Herbert - the letter never came into his father's hands. Why, the reader will learn in the next chapter.

CHAPTER XXXI

THE HOUSEKEEPER'S CRIME

It is not to be supposed that during this time the family of the missing boy were idle. The mystrerious disappearance of his only son filled his father's heart with anguish, and he took immediate steps to penetrate the mystery. Not only was the fullest information given to the police, but an experienced detective connected with a private agency was detailed for the search. The matter also got into the papers, and Herbert, in his Western home, little suspected that his name had already become a household word in thousands of families.

Days passed, and in spite of the efforts that were being made to discover him, no clew had been obtained by Herbert's friends, either as to his whereabouts, or as to the identity of the party or parties hat had abducted him. It is needless to say that Grant heartily sympathized with the afflicted father, and was sad on his own account, for he had become warmly attached to the little boy whose instant companion he had been in his hours of leisure.

The only one in the house who took the matter coolly was Mrs. Estabrook, the housekeeper. She even ventured to suggest that Herbert had run away.

"What do you mean, Mrs. Estabrook?" exclaimed the father, impatiently. "You ought to know my poor boy better than that!"

"Boys are a worrisome set," returned the housekeeper, composedly. "Only last week I read in the Herald about two boys who ran away from good homes and went out to kill Indians."

"Herbert was not that kind of a boy," said Grant. "He had no fondness for adventure."

"I have known Herbert longer than you, young man," retorted the housekeeper, with a sneer.

"It is very clear that you didn't know him as well," said Mr. Reynolds.

Mrs. Estabrook sniffed, but said nothing. Without expressly saying so, it was evident that she dissented from Mr. Reynolds' opinion.

The broker's loss unfitted him for work, and he left the details of office work to his subordinates, while nearly all his time was spent in interviews with the police authorities or in following up faint clews. His loss seemed to strengthen the intimacy and attachment between him and Grant, in whom he confided without reserve. When at home in the evening he talked over with Grant, whom he found a sympathetic listener, the traits of the stolen boy, and brought up reminiscences, trifling, perhaps, but touching, under the circumstances. To Mrs. Estabrook he seldom spoke of his son. Her cold and unsympathetic temperament repelled him. She had never preferred to feel any attachment for Herbert, and the boy, quick to read her want of feeling, never cared to be with her.

One morning, after Mr. Reynolds and Grant had gone out, Mrs. Estabrook, on going to the hall, saw a letter on the table, which had been left by the postman. As curiosity was by no means lacking in the housekeeper's composition, she took it up, and peered at the address through her glasses.

It was directed to Mr. Reynolds in a round, schoolboy hand.

Mrs. Estabrook's heart gave a sudden jump of excitement.

"It's Herbert's handwriting," she said to herself.

She examined the postmark, and found that it was mailed at Scipio, Illinois.

She held the letter in her hand and considered what she should do. Should the letter come into the hands of Mr. Reynolds, the result would doubtless be that the boy would be recovered, and would reveal the name of his abductor. This would subject her favorite, Willis Ford, to arrest, and probably imprisonment.

"He should have been more careful, and not allowed the boy to write," said the housekeeper to herself. "Willis must have been very imprudent. If I only knew what was in the letter!"

The housekeeper's curiosity became so ungovernable that she decided to open it. By steaming it, she could do it, and if it seemed expedient, paste it together again. She had little compunction in the matter. In a few minutes she was able to withdraw the letter from the envelope and read its contents.

This is what Herbert wrote:

"Scipio, ILL.

"DEAR PAPA: I know you must have been very anxious about me. I would have written you before, but I have had no chance. Willis Ford found me playing in the street, and got me to go with him by saying you had sent for me. I thought it strange you should have sent Mr. Ford, but I didn't like to refuse, for fear it was true. We went on board a steamer in the harbor, and Mr. Ford took me in a stateroom. Then he put a handkerchief to my face, and I became sleepy. When I waked up, we were at sea. I don't know where I went, but when we came to land, some time the next day, we got into the cars and traveled for a couple of days. I begged Mr. Ford to take me home, but it made him cross. I think he hates you and Grant, and I think he took me away to spite you. I am sure he is a very wicked man.

"Finally we came to this place. It is a small place in Illinois. The people who live here are Mr. and Mrs. Barton and their son Abner. Mr. Joel Barton is a drunkard. He gets drunk whenever he has money to buy whisky. Mrs. Barton is a hard-working woman, and she does about all the work that is done. Mr. Ford paid her some money in advance. She is a tall woman, and her voice sounds like a man's. She does not ill treat me, but I wish I were at home. Abner is a big, rough boy, a good deal older and larger than I am, but he is kind to me and he wants to come to New York. He says he will run away and take me with him, if we can get enough money to pay our fares. I don't think we could walk it so far. Abner might, for he is a good deal stronger than I am, but I know I should get very tired.

"Now, dear papa, if you will send me money enough to pay for railroad tickets, Abner and I will start just as soon as we get it. I don't know as he ought to run away from home, but he says his father and mother don't care for him, and I don't believe they do. His father doesn't care for anything but whisky, and his mother is scolding him all the time. I don't think she would do that if she cared much for him, do you?

"I have filled the paper, and must stop. Be sure to send the money to your loving son,

"HERBERT REYNOLDS."

"How easy you write!" said Abner, in wonder, as he saw Herbert's letter growing long before his eyes. "It would take me a week to write as long a letter as that, and then I couldn't do it."

"I can't write so easy generally," said the little boy, "but, you see, I have a good deal to write about."

"Then there's another thing," said Abner. "I shouldn't know how to spell so many words. You must be an awful good scholar."

"I always liked to study," said Herbert. "Don't you like to read and study?"

"No; I'd rather play ball or go fishin', wouldn't you?"

"I like to play part of the time, but I wouldn't like to

grow up ignorant."

"I expect I'll always be a know-nothin', but I reckon I know as much as dad. The old man's awful ignorant. He don't care for nothin' but whisky."

"And I hope you won't be like him in that, Abner."

"No, I won't. I wouldn't like to have the boys flingin' stones at me, as they did at dad once when he was tight. I licked a couple of 'em."

Mrs. Estabrook read Herbert's letter with intense interest. She saw that the little boy's testimony would seriously incriminate Willis Ford, if he were recovered, as he would be if this letter came into his father's hands.

"There's only one thing to do," the housekeeper reflected, closing her thin lips tightly.

She lit the gas jet in her chamber, and, without a trace of compunction, held the letter in the flame until it was thoroughly consumed.

CHAPTER XXXII

HOPE DEFERRED

Day after day Herbert and Abner went to the post office and inquired for letters, but alas! none came. Poor Herbert was in despair. He thought his father would have instantly sent the money, or come out himself to take him home. Was it possible his father had forgotten him, or was indifferent to his absence? He could not believe it, but what was he to think?

"I reckon your father didn't get the letter," suggested Abner.

Herbert hailed this suggestion with relief.

"Or, maybe, marm has told the postmaster to give her any letters that come."

This suggestion, too, seemed not improbable.

"What can we do?" asked Herbert, helplessly. "I reckon we'd better run away."

"Without money?"

"We'll hire out to somebody for a week or two and write from where we are."

"I'm afraid I couldn't do much work," said the little boy.

"Then I'll work for both," said Abner, stoutly. "I've got tired of stayin' at home, anyway."

"I'll do whatever you say," said Herbert, feeling that any change would be for the better.

"I'll tell you when I'm ready," said Abner. "We'll start some time when marm's gone to the village."

There was another reason for Herbert's being dissatisfied with his new home. A month had passed - the full time for which Willis Ford had paid the boy's board - and there were no indications that any more was to be paid. During the the first week the fare had been tolerable, though Mrs. Barton was not a skillful cook; but now there was no money left, and the family fell back upon what their limited resources could supply. Mush and milk now constituted their principal diet. It is well enough occasionally, but, when furnished at every meal, both Herbert and Abner became tired of it.

"Haven't you got anything else for dinner, marm?" asked Abner, discontentedly.

"No, I haven't," answered the mother, snappishly.

"You used to have sassiges and bacon."

"That was when I had money to buy 'em."

"Where's all that money gone the man left with him?" indicating Herbert.

"It's spent, and I wish Willis Ford would send along some more mighty quick. He needn't expect me to take a free boarder."

She looked severely at Herbert, as if he were in fault. Certainly the poor boy had no desire to live on the liberality of Mrs. Barton.

"Maybe he's sent you some money in a letter," suggested Abner.

"Well, I never thought of that. It's a bright idee, ef it did come from you, Abner Barton. Jest go up to the postoffice after dinner, and ask if there's any letter for me. Ef there is, mind you, don't open it."

"All right, marm."

"Come along, bub," said Abner.

This was the name he gave to Herbert, whom he liked in his own rough way.

"I don't think," said Herbert, as they walked along, "that your mother can have got any letter written by my father. If she had, she would not be out of money."

"I reckon you're right. Do you think that Ford feller will send money for your board?"

"I think he will, if he can, for he wants to keep me here; but I don't think he has much money with him."

"All the worse for marm."

"Abner," said Herbert, after a pause, during which he

had been thinking seriously, "would you mind running away pretty soon?"

"No, bub; I'm ready any time. Are you in a hurry?"

"You see, Abner, I don't want to live on your mother. She isn't rich -"

"No, I guess not. Ef she hadn't married sech a good-for-nothin' as dad -"

"I wouldn't speak so of your father, Abner."

"Why not? Isn't it the truth? Dad's no grit. He gits drunk whenever he has a chance. Marm's a good, hard-workin' woman. She'd git along well enough ef she was alone."

"At any rate, she can't afford to board me for nothing. So I am ready to start whenever you are, Abner."

"Suppose we get up early to-morror and start?"

"How early?"

"Three o'clock. Marm gets up at five. We must be on the road before that time."

"I'm willing, Abner. You must wake me up in time."

"You'd better go to bed early, bub, and git all the sleep you can. We'll have a hard day to-morrer."

CHAPTER XXXIII

THE JOURNEY BEGINS

"Wake up, there."

The little boy stirred in his sleep, and finally opened his eyes. By the faint light that entered through the window, he saw Abnerbending over him.

"What is it?" he asked, drowsily.

"The kitchen clock's just struck three," whispered Abner. "You haven't forgotten that we are going to run away, have you?"

"I'll get right up," said Herbert, rubbing his eyes.

In two minutes the boys were dressed and ready for a start. It had taken a great deal longer for Herbert to dress at home, but he had become less particular as to his toilet now.

The boys took their shoes in their hands, and stole out in their stocking feet. As they passed the door of the room in which Mr. and Mrs. Barton slept, they heard the deep breathing of both, and knew that they were not likely to be heard.

Outside the door they put on their shoes, and were now ready to start.

"Wait a minute, bub," said Abner.

He re-entered the house, and presently came out holding half a loaf in his hand.

"That'll do for our breakfast," he said. "We won't eat it now. We'll wait till five o'clock. Then we'll be hungry."

By five o'clock they were as many miles on their way. They had reached the middle of the next town.

"Do you feel tired, bub?" asked Abner.

"A little. I feel hungry. Don't you think we can eat the bread now?"

"Yes, we'd better. I feel kind o' gone myself."

They sat down under a tree, and Abner divided the bread fairly.

"You ought to have more than I," protested Herbert. "You're bigger than I, and need more."

"Never mind that! You'll need it to keep up your strength."

Abner was not naturally unselfish, but he was manly enough to feel that he ought to be generous and kind to a boy so much smaller, and he felt repaid for his self-denial by noticing the evident relish with which Herbert ate his allowance of bread, even to the smallest crumb.

They found a spring, which yielded them a cool, refreshing draught, and soon were on their way once more. They had proceeded perhaps two miles further, when the rumbling of wheels was heard behind them, and a farm wagon soon came up alongside. The driver was a man of about thirty - sunburned and roughly clad.

"Whoa, there," he said.

The horse stopped.

"Where are you two goin'?" he asked.

"We're travelin'," answered Abner, noncommittally.

"Where's your home?"

"Some ways back."

"Where are you goin'?"

"I'm after work," answered Abner.

"Well, you'd orter be a good hand at it. You look strong. Is that little feller your brother?"

"No; he's my cousin."

Herbert looked up in surprise at this avowal of relationship, but he thought it best not to say anything that would conflict with Abner's statement.

"Is he after work, too?" asked the driver, with a smile.

"No; he's goin' to his father."

"Where does he live?"

"Further on."

"Have you walked fur?"

"Pretty fur."

"Ef you want to ride, I'll give you a lift for a few miles."

"Thank you," said Abner, prompt to accept the offer. "I'll help you in, bub."

The two boys took their seats beside the driver, Herbert being in the middle. The little boy was really tired, and he found it very pleasant to ride, instead of walking. He had walked seven miles already, and that was more than he had ever before walked at one time.

They rode about three miles, when the driver pulled up in front of a comfortable-looking house.

"This is where I stop," he said. "My aunt lives here, and my sister has been paying her a visit. I've come to take her home."

The front door was opened, and his aunt and sister came out.

"You're just in time for breakfast, John," said his aunt. "Come in and sit down to the table. Bring in the boys, too."

"Come in, boys," said the young man. "I guess you can eat something, can't you?"

"We've had -" Herbert began, but Abner checked him.

"Come along, bub," he said. "What's a bit of bread? I ain't half full."

CHAPTER XXIV

MRS. BARTON'S SURPRISE

A hearty breakfast, consisting of beefsteak, potatoes, corn bread, fresh butter and apple sauce, made Abner's eyes glisten, for he had never in his remembrance sat down at home to a meal equally attractive. He wielded his knife and fork with an activity and energy which indicated thorough enjoyment. Even Herbert, though in the city his appetite had been delicate, and he had already eaten part of a loaf of bread, did excellent justice to the good things set before him. He was himself surprised at his extraordinary appetite, forgetting the stimulating effect of a seven-mile walk.

After breakfast they set out again on their tramp. At sunset, having rested several hours in the middle of the day, they had accomplished twenty miles. Abner could have gone further, but Herbert was well tired out. They obtained permission from a friendly farmer to spend the night in his barn, and retired at half-past seven. Mr. Reynolds would have been shocked had he known that his little son was compelled to sleep on a pile of hay, but it may truthfully be said that Herbert had seldom slept as soundly or felt more refreshed.

"How did you sleep, Abner?" he asked.

"Like a top. How was it with you, bub?"

"I didn't wake up all night," answered the little boy.

"I wonder what dad and marm thought when they found us gone?" said Abner, with a grin.

"Won't they feel bad?"

"Not much," said Abner. "They ain't that kind. I reckon it won't spoil their appetite."

When they descended from the haymow, the farmer was milking his cows.

"Well, youngsters," he said, "so you're up and dressed?"

"Yes, sir."

"And ready for breakfast, I'll be bound."

"I reckon I should feel better for eatin'," said Abner, promptly.

"Jest you wait till I get through milkin', and we'll see what Mrs. Wiggins has got for us."

Abner heard these words with joy, for he was always possessed of a good appetite.

"I say, bub, I'm glad I run away," he remarked, aside, to Herbert. "We live enough sight better than we did at home."

Leaving the boys to pursue their journey, we will

return to the bereaved parents, and inquire how they bore their loss.

When Mrs. Barton rose to commence the labors of the day, she found that no wood was on hand for the kitchen fire.

"Abner's gittin' lazier and lazier," she soliloquized. "I'll soon have him up."

She went to the foot of the stairs, and called "Abner!" in a voice by no means low or gentle.

There was no answer.

"That boy would sleep if there was an earthquake," she muttered. "Come down here and split some wood, you lazy boy!" she cried, still louder.

Again no answer.

"He hears, fast enough, but he don't want to work. I'll soon have him down."

She ascended the stairs, two steps at a time, and opened the door of her son's room.

If Abner had been in bed his mother would have pulled him out, for her arm was vigorous, but the bed was empty.

"Well, I vum!" she ejaculated, in surprise. "Ef that boy isn't up already. That's a new wrinkle. And the little boy gone, too. What can it mean?"

It occurred to Mrs. Barton that Abner and Herbert

might have got up early to go fishing, though she had never known him to make so early a start before.

"I reckon breakfast'll bring 'em round," she said to herself. "I reckon I shall have to split the wood myself."

In half an hour breakfast was ready. It was of a very simple character, for the family resources were limited. Mr. Barton came downstairs, and looked discontentedly at the repast provided.

"This is a pretty mean breakfast, Mrs. B.," he remarked. "Where's your meat and taters?"

"There's plenty of 'em in the market," answered Mrs. Barton.

"Then, why didn't you buy some?"

"You ought to know, Joel Barton. You give me the money, and I'll see that you have a good breakfast."

"Where's all the money that man Ford gave you?"

"Where is it? It's eaten up, Mr. Barton, and you did your share. Ef you'd had your way, you'd have spent some of the money for drink."

"Why don't he send you some more, then?"

"Ef you see him anywheres, you'd better ask him. It's your business to provide me with money; you can't expect one boy's board to support the whole family."

"It's strange where them boys are gone," said Joel,

desirous of changing the subject. "Like as not, they hid under the bed, and fooled you."

"Ef they did, I'll rout 'em out," said Mrs. Barton, who thought the supposition not improbable.

Once more she ascended the stairs and made an irruption into the boy's chamber. She lifted the quilt, and peered under the bed. But there were no boys there. Looking about the room, however, she discovered something else. On the mantelpiece was a scrap of paper, which appeared to be so placed as to invite attention.

"What's that?" said Mrs. Barton to herself.

A moment later she was descending the staircase more rapidly than she had gone up just before.

"Look at that," she exclaimed, holding out a scrap of paper to Joel Barton.

"I don't see nothin' but a bit of paper," said her husband.

"Don't be a fool! Read what it is."

"Read it aloud. I ain't got my specks."

"The boys have run away. Abner writ it. Listen to this."

Rudely written on the paper, for Abner was by no means a skillful penman, were these words:

"Bub and I have runned away. You needn't worry. I

reckon we can get along. We're going to make our fortunes. When we're rich, we'll come back. ABNER."

"What do you think of that, Joel Barton?" demanded his wife.

Joel shrugged his shoulders.

"I shan't worry much," he said. "They'll be back by to-morrer, likely."

"Then you'll have to split some wood to-day, Joel. You can't expect a delicate woman like me to do such rough work."

"You're stronger'n I be, Mrs. B."

"Perhaps you'll find I am if you don't go to work."

"I'll do it this afternoon."

"All right. Then we'll have dinner in the even-in'. No wood, no dinner."

"Seems to me you're rather hard on me, Mrs. B. I don't feel well."

"Nor you won't till you give up drinkin'."

Much against his will, Mr. Barton felt compelled by the stress of circumstances to do the work expected of him. It made him feel angry with Abner, whom he did not miss for any other reason.

"I'll break that boy's neck when he comes back," he muttered. "It's a shame to leave all this work for his poor, old dad."

To-morrow came, but the boys did not. A week slipped away, and still they were missing. Mrs. Barton was not an affectionate mother, but it did seem lonesome without Abner. As for Herbert, she did not care for his absence. If Willis Ford did not continue to pay his board, she felt that she would rather have him away.

On the sixth day after the departure of the boys there came a surprise for Mrs. Barton.

As she was at work in the kitchen, she heard a loud knock at the door.

"Can it be Abner?" she thought. "He wouldn't knock."

She went to the door, however, feeling rather curious as to who could be her visitor, and on opening it started in surprise to see Willis Ford.

"Mr. Ford!" she ejaculated.

"I thought I would make you a call," answered Ford. "How's the boy getting along?"

"If you mean the boy you left here," she answered, composedly, "he's run away, and took my boy with him."

"Run away!" ejaculated Ford, in dismay.

"Yes; he made tracks about a week ago. He and my Abner have gone off to make their fortunes."

"Why didn't you take better care of him, woman?"

exclaimed Ford, angrily. "It's your fault, his running away!"

"Look here, Ford," retorted Mrs. Barton; "don't you sass me, for I won't stand it. Ef it hadn't been for you, Abner would be at home now."

"I didn't mean to offend you, my dear Mrs. Barton," said Ford, seeing that he had made a false step. "Tell me all you can, and I'll see if I can't get the boys back."

"Now you're talkin'," said Mrs. Barton, smoothing her ruffled plumage. "Come into the house, and I'll tell you all I know."

CHAPTER XXXV

HERBERT BREAKS DOWN

"I don't think I can walk any further, Abner. I feel sick," faltered Herbert.

Abner, who had been walking briskly, turned round to look at his young companion. Herbert was looking very pale, and had to drag one foot after the other. Day after day he had tried to keep up with Abner, but his strength was far inferior to that of the other boy, and he had finally broken down.

"You do look sick, bub," said Abner, struck by Herbert's pallid look. "Was I walking too fast for you?"

"I feel very weak," said Herbert. "Would you mind stopping a little while? I should like to lie under a tree and rest."

"All right, bub. There's a nice tree." "Don't you feel tired, Abner?"

"No; I feel as strong as hearty as a horse."

"You are bigger than I am. I guess that is the reason."

Abner was a rough boy, but he showed unusual

gentleness and consideration for the little boy, whose weakness appealed to his better nature. He picked out a nice, shady place for Herbert to recline upon, and, taking off his coat, laid it down for a pillow on which his young companion might rest his head.

"There, bub; I reckon you'll feel better soon," he said.

"I hope so, Abner. I wish I was as strong as you are."

"So do I. I reckon I was born tough. I was brought up different from you."

"I wish I were at home," sighed Herbert. "Is it a long way from here?"

"I reckon it is, but I don't know," answered Abner, whose geographical notions were decidedly hazy.

An hour passed, and still Herbert lay almost motionless, as if rest were a luxury, with his eyes fixed thoughtfully upon the clouds that could be seen through the branches floating lazily above.

"Don't you feel any better, bub?" asked Abner.

"I feel better while I am lying here, Abner."

"Don't you feel strong enough to walk a little further?"

"Must I?" asked Herbert, sighing. "It is so nice to lie here."

"I am afraid we shall never get to New York if we don't keep goin'."

"I'll try," said Herbert, and he rose to his feet, but he only staggered and became very white.

"I am afraid I need to rest a little more," he said.

"All right, bub. Take your time."

More critically Abner surveyed his young companion. He was not used to sickness or weakness, but there was something in the little boy's face that startled him.

"I don't think you're fit to walk any further today," he said. "I wish we had some good place to stay."

At this moment a carriage was seen approaching. It was driven by a lady of middle age, with a benevolent face. Her attention was drawn to the two boys, and especially to Herbert. Her experienced eyes at once saw that he was sick.

She halted her horse.

"What is the matter with your brother?" she said to Abner.

"I reckon he's tuckered out," said Abner, tacitly admitting the relationship. "We've been travelin' for several days. He ain't so tough as I am."

"He looks as if he were going to be sick. Have you any friends near here?"

"No, ma'am. The nighest is over a hundred miles off."

The lady reflected a moment. Then she said: "I think you had better come to my house. My brother is a doctor. He will look at your little brother and see what can be done for him."

"I should like it very much," said Abner, "but we haven't got any money to pay for doctors and sich."

"I shan't present any bill, nor will my brother," said the lady, smiling. "Do you think you can help him into the carriage?"

"Oh, yes, ma'am."

Abner helped Herbert into the carriage, and then, by invitation, got in himself.

"May I drive?" he asked, eagerly.

"Yes, if you like."

The kind lady supported with her arm Herbert's drooping head, and so they drove on for a mile, when she indicated that they were to stop in front of a large, substantial, square house, built after the New England style.

Herbert was taken out, and, after Abner helped him upstairs, into a large, square chamber, with four windows.

"What is his name?" asked the lady.

"Herbert."

"And yours?"

"Abner."

"He had better lie down on the bed, and, as soon as my brother comes, I will send him up."

Herbert breathed a sigh of satisfaction, as he reclined on the comfortable bed, which was more like the one he slept in at home than the rude, straw bed which he had used when boarding with Mr. and Mrs. Barton.

Half an hour passed, and the doctor came into the room, and felt Herbert's pulse.

"The boy is tired out," he said. "That is all. His strength has been exhausted by too severe physical effort."

"What shall we do to bring him round?" asked his sister.

"Rest and nourishing food are all that is required."

"Shall we keep him here? Have you any objection?"

"I should object to letting him go in his present condition. He will be a care to you, Emily."

"I shall not mind that. We shall have to keep the other boy, too."

"Certainly. There's room enough for both."

When Abner was told that for a week to come they were to stay in Dr. Stone's comfortable house, his face indicated his satisfaction.

"Ef you've got any chores to do, ma'am," he said, "I'll do 'em. I'm strong, and not afraid to work."

"Then I will make you very useful," said Miss Stone, smiling.

The next day, as she was sitting in Herbert's chamber, she said: "Herbert, you don't look at all like your brother."

"Do you mean Abner, Miss Stone?" Herbert asked.

"Yes; have you any other brother?"

"Abner is not my brother at all."

"How, then, do you happen to be traveling together?"

"Because we've both run away."

"I am sorry to hear that. I don't approve of boys running away. Where do you live?"

"In New York."

"In New York!" repeated Miss Stone, much surprised. "Surely, you have not walked from there?"

"No, Miss Stone; I was stolen from my home in New York about a month ago, and left at Abner's house. It was a poor cabin, and very different from anything I was accustomed to. I did not like Mr. and Mrs. Barton; but Abner was always kind to me."

"Is your father living?" asked Miss Stone, who had become interested.

"Yes; he is a broker."

"And no doubt you have a nice home?"

"Yes, very nice. It is a brownstone house uptown. I wonder whether I shall ever see it again?"

"Surely you will. I am surprised that you have not written to tell your father where you are. He must be feeling very anxious about you."

"I did write, asking him to send me money to come home. Abner was going with me. But no answer came to my letter."

"That is strange. Your father can't have received the letter."

"So I think, Miss Stone; but I directed it all right."

"Do you think any one would intercept it?"

"Mrs. Estabrook might," said Herbert, after a pause for consideration.

"Who is she?"

"The housekeeper."

"What makes you think so? Didn't she like you?"

"No; besides, it was her nephew who carried me off."

Miss Stone asked further questions, and Herbert told her all the particulars with which the reader is already acquainted. When he had finished, she said: "My advice is, that you write to your boy friend, Grant Thornton, or tell me what to write, and I will write to him. His letters will not be likely to be tampered with."

"I think that will be a good idea," said Herbert; "Grant will tell papa, and then he'll send for me."

Miss Stone brought her desk to the bedside, and wrote a letter to Grant at Herbert's dictation. This letter she sent to the village postoffice immediately by Abner.

CHAPTER XXXVI

GRANT RECEIVES A LETTER

Mr. Reynolds had spared no expense in his efforts to obtain tidings of his lost boy. None of his agents, however, had succeeded in gaining the smallest clew to Herbert's whereabouts. Through the public press the story had been widely disseminated, and in consequence the broker began to receive letters from various points, from persons professing to have seen such a boy as the one described. One of these letters came from Augusta, Ga., and impressed Mr. Reynolds to such an extent that he decided to go there in person, and see for himself the boy of whom his correspondent wrote.

The day after he started Grant, on approaching the house at the close of business, fell in with the postman, just ascending the steps.

"Have you got a letter for me?" he asked.

"I have a letter for Grant Thornton," was the reply.

"That is my name," said Grant.

He took the letter, supposing it to be from home. He was surprised to find that it had a Western postmark.

He was more puzzled by the feminine handwriting.

"Have you heard anything from the little boy?" asked the postman, for Mr. Reynolds' loss was well known.

Grant shook his head.

"Nothing definite," he said. "Mr. Reynolds has gone to Georgia to follow up a clew."

"Two weeks since," said the postman, "I left a letter here dated at Scipio, I11. It was in a boy's handwriting. I thought it might be from the lost boy."

"A letter from Scipio, in a boy's handwriting!" repeated Grant, surprised. "Mr. Reynolds has shown me all his letters. He has received none from there."

"I can't understand it. I left it here, I am positive of that."

"At what time in the day?" asked Grant, quickly.

"About eleven o'clock in the forenoon."

"Can you tell to whom you gave it?"

"To the servant."

"It is very strange," said Grant, thoughtfully. "And it was in a boy's handwriting?"

"Yes; the address was in a round, schoolboy hand. The servant couldn't have lost it, could she?"

"No; Sarah is very careful."

"Well, I must be going."

By this time Grant had opened the letter. He had glanced rapidly at the signature, and his face betrayed excitement.

"This is from Herbert," he said. "You may listen, if you like."

He rapidly read the letter, which in part was as follows:

"DEAR GRANT: I write to you, or rather I have asked Miss Stone, who is taking care of me, to do so, because I wrote to papa two weeks since, and I am afraid he did not get the letter, for I have had no answer. I wrote from the town of Scipio, in Illinois -

"Just what I said," interrupted the postman.

"I wrote that Mr. Ford had carried me away and brought me out West, where he put me to board in a poor family, where I had scarcely enough to eat. Mr. Barton had one son, Abner, who treated me well, and agreed to run away with me to New York, if we could get money from papa. But we waited and waited, and no letter came. So at last we decided to run away at any rate, for I was afraid Mr. Ford would come back and take me somewhere else. I can't tell you much about the journey, except that we walked most of the way, and we got very tired - or, at least, I did, for I am not so strong as Abner - till I broke down. I am stopping now at the house of Dr. Stone, who is very kind, and so is his sister, who is writing this letter for me. Will you show papa this letter, and ask him to send for me, if he cannot come himself? I do so long to be at home once more. I hope he will come before Willis

Ford finds me out. I think he has a spite against papa, and that is why he stole me away. Your affectionate friend,

"HERBERT REYNOLDS."

"Please say nothing about this," said Grant to the postman. "I don't want it known that this letter has come."

"What will you do?"

"I shall start for the West myself to-night."

"Mrs. Estabrook intercepted that letter," said Grant to himself. "I am sure of it."

CHAPTER XXXVII

WILLIS FORD FINDS THE RUNAWAYS

"I shall be absent for a few days, Mrs. Estabrook," said Grant to the housekeeper, as he entered the house.

"Where are you going?" she inquired.

"I can't tell you definitely."

"Hadn't you better wait till Mr. Reynolds gets back?"

"No; business is not very pressing in the office, and I can be spared."

The housekeeper concluded that Grant was going to Colebrook, and did not connect his journey with the lost boy.

"Oh, well, I suppose you understand your own business best. Herbert will miss you if he finds you away when his father brings him back."

"Do you think he will?" asked Grant, eyeing the housekeeper sharply.

"I'm sure I don't know. I suppose he expects to, or he would not have traveled so far in search of him."

"Shall you be glad to see him back, Mrs. Estabrook?"

"Of course! What makes you doubt it?" demanded the housekeeper, sharply.

"I thought you didn't like Herbert."

"I wasn't always petting him. It isn't in my way to pet boys."

"Do you often hear from Willis Ford?"

"That is my business," answered Mrs. Estabrook, sharply. "Why do you ask?"

"I was wondering whether he knew that Herbert had been abducted."

"That is more than we know. Very likely the boy ran away."

Grant called on the cashier at his private residence, confided to him his plan, and obtained a sum of money for traveling expenses. He left the Grand Central Depot by the evening train, and by morning was well on his way to Chicago.

Meanwhile, Willis Ford had left no stone unturned to obtain news of the runaways. This he did not find difficult, though attended with delay. He struck the right trail, and then had only to inquire, as he went along, whether two boys had been seen, one small and delicate, the other large and well-grown, wandering through the country. Plenty had seen the two boys, and told him so.

"Are they your sons, mister?" asked a laborer of whom he inquired.

"Not both of them - only the smaller," answered Ford, with unblushing falsehood.

"And what made them run away now?"

"My son probably did not like the boarding place I selected for him."

"Why didn't he write to you?"

"He didn't know where to direct."

"Who is the other lad?"

"The son of the man I placed him with. I think he may have induced Sam to run away."

Finally Ford reached Claremont, the town where the boys had actually found refuge. Here he learned that two boys had been taken in by Dr. Stone, answering to the description he gave. One, the younger one, had been sick, but now was better. This information he obtained at the hotel.

Ford's eyes sparkled with exultation. He had succeeded in his quest, and once more Herbert was in his hands, or would be very soon.

He inquired the way to Dr. Stone's. Everybody knew where the doctor lived, and he had no trouble in securing the information he sought. Indeed, before he reached the house, he caught sight of Abner, walking in the same direction with himself, but a few rods ahead.

He quickened his pace, and laid his hand on the boy's shoulder.

Abner turned, and an expression of dismay overspread his face.

"Ha, my young friend! I see that you remember me," said Ford, ironically.

"Well, what do you want?" asked Abner, sullenly.

"You know well enough. I want the boy you have persuaded to run away with you."

"I didn't persuade him."

"Never mind about quibbling. I know where the boy is, and I mean to have him."

"Do you want me, too?"

"No; I don't care where you go."

"I reckon Herbert won't go with you."

"And I reckon he will. That is Dr. Stone's, isn't it? Never mind answering. I know well enough it is."

"He'll have bub sure," said Abner, disconsolately. "But I'll follow 'em, and I'll get him away, as sure as my name's Abner Barton."

CHAPTER XXXVIII

FORD TAKES A BOLD STEP, BUT FAILS

"I wish to see Miss Stone," said Willis Ford, to the servant.

"I'll tell her. What name shall I say?"

"Never mind about the name. I wish to see her on business of importance."

"I don't like his looks," thought the maid. "Shure he talks as if he was the boss."

She told Miss Stone, however, that a gentleman wished to see her, who would not tell his name.

Miss Stone was in Herbert's chamber, and the boy - now nearly well, quite well, in fact, but for a feeling of languor and weakness - heard the message.

"What is he like?" he asked, anxiously.

"He's slender like, with black hair and a black mustache, and he talks like he was the master of the house."

"I think it is Willis Ford," said Herbert, turning pale.

"The man who abducted you?" ejaculated Miss Stone.

"Yes, the same man. Don't let him take me away," implored Herbert.

"I wish my brother were here," said Miss Stone, anxiously.

"Won't he be here soon?"

"I am afraid not. He has gone on a round of calls. Bridget, tell the young man I will be down directly."

Five minutes later Miss Stone descended, and found Willis Ford fuming with impatience.

"I am here, sir," she said, coldly. "I understand you wish to see me."

"Yes, madam; will you answer me a few questions?"

"Possibly. Let me hear what they are."

"You have a boy in this house, named Herbert Reynolds?"

"Yes."

"A boy who ran away from Mr. Joel Barton, with whom I placed him?"

"What right had you to place him anywhere, Mr. Ford?" demanded the lady.

"That's my business. Permit me to say that it is no affair of yours."

"I judge differently. The boy is sick and under my charge."

"I am his natural guardian, madam."

"Who made you so, Mr. Ford?"

"I shall not argue that question. It is enough that I claim him as my cousin and ward."

"Your cousin?"

"Certainly. That doubtless conflicts with what he has told you. He was always a liar."

"His story is, that you beguiled him from his home in New York, and brought him against his will to this part of the country."

"And you believe him?" sneered Ford.

"I do."

"It matters little whether you do or not. He is my sister's child, and is under my charge. I thought fit to place him with Mr. Joel Barton, of Scipio, but the boy, who is flighty, was induced to run away with Barton's son, a lazy, shiftless fellow."

"Supposing this to be so, Mr. Ford, what is your object in calling?"

"To reclaim him. It does not suit me to leave him here."

Ford's manner was so imperative that Miss Stone

became alarmed.

"The boy is not fit to travel," she said. "Wait till my brother comes, and he will decide, being a physician, whether it is safe to have him go."

"Madam, this subterfuge will not avail," said Ford, rudely. "I will not wait till your brother comes. I prefer to take the matter into my own hands."

He pressed forward to the door of the room, and before Miss Stone could prevent it, was on his way upstairs. She followed as rapidly as she could, but before she could reach him, Ford had dashed into the room where Herbert lay on the bed.

Herbert was stricken with terror when he saw the face of his enemy.

"I see you know me," said Ford, with an evil smile. "Get up at once, and prepare to go with me."

"Leave me here, Mr. Ford. I can't go with you; Indeed, I can't," said Herbert.

"We'll see about that," said Ford. "I give you five minutes to rise and put on your clothes. If you don't obey me, I will flog you."

Looking into his cruel face, Herbert felt that he had no other resource. Trembling, he slipped out of bed, and began to draw on his clothes. He felt helpless, but help was nearer than he dreamed.

"Mr. Ford, I protest against this high-handed proceeding," exclaimed Miss Stone, indignantly, as she appeared at the door of the chamber. "What right have you to go over my house without permission?"

"If it comes to that," sneered Ford, "what right have you to keep my ward from me?"

"I am not his ward," said Herbert, quickly.

"The boy is a liar," exclaimed Ford, harshly.

"Get back into the bed, Herbert," said Miss Stone. "This man shall not take you away."

"Perhaps you will tell me how you are going to help it," retorted Ford, with an evil smile.

"If my brother were here -"

"But your brother is not here, and if he were, I would not allow him to interfere between me and my cousin. Herbert, unless you continue dressing, I shall handle you roughly."

But sounds were heard upon the stairs, and Ford, as well as Miss Stone, turned their eyes to the door.

The first to enter was Abner.

"Oh, it's you, is it?" said Ford, contemptuously.

He had thought it might be Dr. Stone, whom he was less inclined to face than he professed.

"Yes, it is. What are you doing here?"

"It is none of your business, you cub. He's got to come

with me."

"Maybe you want me, too?"

"I wouldn't take you as a gift."

"Ho, ho," laughed Abner, "I reckon you'd find me a tough customer. You won't take bub, either."

"Who is to prevent me?"

"I will!" said a new voice, and Grant Thornton, who had fallen in with Abner outside, walked quietly into the room.

Willis Ford started back in dismay. Grant was the last person he expected to meet here. He had no idea that any one of the boy's home friends had tracked him this far. He felt that he was defeated, but he hated to acknowledge it.

"How are you going to prevent me, you young whippersnapper?" he said, glaring menacingly at Grant.

"Mr. Willis Ford, unless you leave this room and this town at once," said Grant, firmly, "I will have you arrested. There is a local officer below whom I brought with me, suspecting your object in coming here."

"Oh, Grant, how glad I am to see you! Is papa with you?" exclaimed Herbert, overjoyed.

"I will tell you about it soon, Herbert."

"You won't let him take me away?"

"There is no danger of that," said Grant, reassuringly. "I shall take you home to New York as soon as this good lady says you are well enough to go."

Ford stood gnawing his nether lip. If it had been Mr. Reynolds, he would not have minded so much; but for a mere boy, like Grant Thornton, to talk with such a calm air of superiority angered him.

"Boy," he said, "it sounds well for you to talk of arrest - you who stole my aunt's bonds, and are indebted to her forbearance for not being at this moment in State's prison."

"Your malicious charge does not affect me, Mr. Ford," returned Grant. "It was proved before you left New York that you were the thief, and even your stepmother must have admitted it. Mr. Reynolds discharged you from his employment, and this is the mean revenge you have taken - the abduction of his only son."

"I will do you an injury yet, you impudent boy," said Ford, furiously.

"I shall be on my guard, Mr. Ford," answered Grant. "I believe you capable of it."

"Don't you think you had better leave us, sir?" said Miss Stone.

"I shall take my own time about going," he answered, impudently.

But his words were heard by Dr. Stone, who had returned sooner than he anticipated, and was already at the door of the room. He was a powerful man, and of quick temper. His answer was to seize Ford by the collar and fling him downstairs.

"This will teach you to be more polite to a lady," he said. "Now, what does all this mean, and who is this man?"

The explanation was given.

"I wish I had been here before," said the doctor.

"You were in good time," said Grant, smiling. "I see that Herbert has found powerful friends."

Willis Ford, angry and humiliated, picked himself up, but did not venture to return to the room he had left so ignominiously. Like most bullies, he was a coward, and he did not care to encounter the doctor again.

Within an hour, Grant telegraphed to the broker at his office: "I have found Herbert, and will start for New York with him to-morrow." Mr. Reynolds had only just returned from his fruitless Southern expedition, weary and dispirited. But he forgot all his fatigue when he read this message. "God bless Grant Thornton!" he ejaculated.

CHAPTER XXXIX

THE HOUSEKEEPER'S RETRIBUTION

The train from Chicago had just reached the Grand Central Depot. From the parlor car descended two boys who are well known to us, Grant Thornton and Herbert Reynolds.

Herbert breathed a sigh of satisfaction.

"Oh, Grant," he said, "how glad I am to see New York once more! I wonder if papa knows we are to come by this train?"

The answer came speedily.

The broker, who had just espied them, hurried forward, and his lost boy was lifted to his embrace.

"Thank God, I have recovered you, my dear son," he exclaimed, fervently.

"You must thank Grant, too, papa," said the little boy. "It was he who found me and prevented Mr. Ford stealing me again."

Mr. Reynolds grasped Grant's hand and pressed it warmly.

"I shall know how to express my gratitude to Grant in due time," he said.

On their way home Grant revealed to Mr. Reynolds for the first time the treachery of the housekeeper, who had suppressed Herbert's letter to his father, and left the latter to mourn for his son when she might have relieved him of the burden of sorrow.

As Mr. Reynolds listened, his face became stern.

"That woman is a viper!" he said. "In my house she has enjoyed every comfort and every consideration, and in return she has dealt me this foul blow. She will have cause to regret it."

When they entered the house Mrs. Estabrook received them with false smiles.

"So you are back again, Master Herbert," she said. "A fine fright you gave us!"

"You speak as if Herbert went away of his own accord," said the broker sternly. "You probably know better."

"I know nothing, sir, about it."

"Then I may inform you that it was your stepson, Willis Ford, who stole my boy - a noble revenge, truly, upon me for discharging him."

"I don't believe it," said the housekeeper. "I presume it is your office boy who makes this charge?" she added, pressing her thin lips together.

"There are others who are cognizant of it, Mrs. Estabrook. Grant succeeded in foiling Mr. Ford in his attempt to recover Herbert, who had run away from his place of confinement,"

"You are prejudiced against my son, Mr. Reynolds," said Mrs. Estabrook, her voice trembling with anger.

"Not more than against you, Mrs. Estabrook. I have a serious charge to bring against you."

"What do you mean, sir?" asked the housekeeper, nervously.

"Why did you suppress the letter which my boy wrote to me revealing his place of imprisonment?"

"I don't know what you mean, sir," she answered, half defiantly.

"I think you do."

"Did Master Herbert write such a letter?" "Yes."

"Then it must have miscarried."

"On the contrary, the postman expressly declares that he delivered it at this house. I charge you with concealing or suppressing it."

"The charge is false. You can't prove it, sir."

"I shall not attempt to do so; but I am thoroughly convinced of it. After this act of treachery, I cannot permit you to spend another night in my house. You will please pack at once, and arrange for a removal."

"I am entitled to a month's notice, Mr. Reynolds."

"You shall have a month's wages in lieu of it. I would as soon have a serpent in my house."

Mrs. Estabrook turned pale. She had never expected it would come to this. She thought no one would ever be able to trace the suppressed letter to her. She was not likely again to obtain so comfortable and desirable a position. Instead of attributing her ill fortune to her own malice and evil doing, she chose to attribute it to Grant.

"I am to thank you for this, Grant Thornton," she said, in sudden passion. "I was right in hating you as soon as I first saw you. If ever I am able I will pay you up for this."

"I don't doubt it, Mrs. Estabrook," said Grant, quietly, "but I don't think you will have it in your power."

She did not deign to answer, but hurried out of the room. In half an hour she had left the house.

"Now I can breathe freely," said the broker. "That woman was so full of malice and spite that it made me uncomfortable to feel that she was in the house."

"I am so glad that she has gone, papa," said Herbert.

That evening, after Herbert had gone to bed, Mr. Reynolds invited Grant into his library.

"My boy," he said, "I have settled accounts with Mrs. Estabrook; now I want to settle with you."

"Not in the same way, I hope, sir," said Grant.

"Yes, in the same way, according to your deserts. You have done me a service, that which none can be greater. You have been instrumental in restoring to me my only son."

"I don't want any reward for that, sir."

"Perhaps not; but I owe it to myself to see that this service is acknowledged. I shall raise your salary to fifteen dollars a week."

"Thank you, sir," said Grant, joyfully. "How glad my mother will be."

"When you tell her this, you may also tell her that I have deposited on your account in the Bowery Savings Bank the sum of five thousand dollars."

"This is too much, Mr. Reynolds," said Grant, quite overwhelmed. "Why, I shall feel like a man of fortune."

"So you will be in time, if you continue as faithful to business as in the past."

"It seems to me like a dream," said Grant.

"I will give you a week's leave of absence to visit your parents, and tell them of your good fortune."

CHAPTER XL

CONCLUSION

There were anxious hearts in the parsonage at Colebrook. For some weeks the minister had shown signs of overwork. His appetite had failed, and he seemed weary and worn.

"He needs change," said the doctor. "A run over to Europe would do him good. He has no disease; he only wants change."

"A trip to Europe," said Mr. Thornton, shaking his head. "It is impossible. It has been the dream of my life, but a country minister could not, in half a dozen years, save money enough for that."

"If your brother Godfrey would lend you the money, Grant might, in time, help you to pay it."

Godfrey never had forgiven Grant for running counter to his plans.

"I wish I could spare the money myself, Mr. Thornton," said the doctor. "Five hundred dollars would be sufficient, and it would make a new man of you."

"It might as well be five thousand," said the minister,

shaking his head. "No, my good friend, I must toil on as well as I can, and leave European trips to more favored men."

It was noised about through the parish that the minister was sick, and the doctor recommended a European trip.

"It's ridikilus," was Deacon Gridley's comment. "I work harder than the minister, and I never had to go to Europe. It's just because it's fashionable."

"Mr. Thornton is looking pale and haggard," said Mrs. Gridley.

"What if he is? He ought to work outdoors like me. Then he'd know what work was. Ac-cordin' to my notion, ministers have a pooty easy time."

Mr. Tudor was of the same opinion.

"It's all nonsense, deacon," he said. "Father wanted me to be a minister, and I'd have had a good deal easier time if I had followed his advice."

"You wouldn't have had so much money, Mr. Tudor," said Miss Lucretia Spring, who heard this remark.

"Mebbe not; but what I've got I've worked for."

"For my part, although I am not near as rich as you are, I'd give twenty dollars toward sending the minister abroad," said kindly Miss Spring.

"I wouldn't give a cent," said Mr. Tudor, with emphasis.

"Nor I," said Deacon Gridley. "I don't believe in humorin' the clergy."

Saturday came, and the minister was worse. It seemed doubtful if he would be able to officiate the next day. No wonder he became dispirited.

Just before supper the stage drove up to the door, and Grant jumped out.

"I am afraid he has been discharged," said Mr. Thornton, nervously.

"He does not look like it," said Mrs. Thornton, noticing Grant's beaming countenance.

"What is the matter with father?" asked Grant, stopping short as he entered.

"He is not feeling very well, Grant. He has got run down."

"What does the doctor say?"

"He says your father ought to take a three-months trip to Europe."

"Which, of course, is impossible," said Mr. Thornton, smiling faintly.

"Not if your brother would open his heart, and lend you the money."

"He would not do it."

"And we won't ask him," said Grant, quickly, "but you

shall go, all the same, father."

"My son, it would cost five hundred dollars."

"And for twice as much, mother, could go with you; you would need her to take care of you. Besides she needs a change, too."

"It is a pleasant plan, Grant; but we must not think of it."

"That's where I don't agree with you. You and mother shall go as soon as you like, and I will pay the expenses."

"Is the boy crazy?" said the minister.

"I'll answer that for myself, father. I have five thousand dollars in the Bowery Savings Bank, in New York, and I don't think I can spend a part of it better than in giving you and mother a European trip."

Then the explanation came, and with some difficulty the minister was made to understand that the dream of his life was to be realized, and that he and his wife were really going to Europe.

"Well, well! who'd have thought it?" ejaculated Deacon Gridley. "That boy of the minister's must be plaguey smart. I never thought he'd be so successful. All the same, it seems to me a mighty poor investment to spend a thousand dollars on racin' to Europe. That money would buy quite a sizable farm."

Others, however, less narrow in their notions, heartily approved of the European trip. When three months later the minister came home, he looked like a new man. His eye was bright, his face bronzed and healthy, his step elastic, and he looked half a dozen years younger.

"This all comes of having a good son," he said, smiling, in reply to congratulations, "a son who, in helping himself, has been alive to help others."

Half a dozen years have passed. Grant Thornton is now a young man, and junior partner of Mr. Reynolds. He has turned his money to good account, and is counted rich for one of his age. He has renewed his acquaintance with Miss Carrie Clifton, whom he met for the first time as a summer boarder in Colebrook, and from their intimacy it wouldn't be surprising if Grant should some day become the wealthy jeweler's son-in-law.

Uncle Godfrey has become reconciled to Grant's following his own course. It is easy to become reconciled to success.

Willis Ford is confined in a penitentiary in a Western State, having been convicted of forgery, and there is small chance of his amendment. He has stripped his stepmother of her last penny, and she is compelled to live on the charity of a relative, who accords her a grudging welcome, and treats her with scant consideration. The bitterest drop in her cup of humiliation is the prosperity of Grant Thornton, toward whom she feels a fierce and vindictive hatred. As she has sown, so she reaps. Malice and uncharitableness seldom bring forth welcome fruit.

www.ingramcontent.com/pod-product-compliance
Lightning Source LLC
LaVergne TN
LVHW090558110826
845146LV00001B/172

* 9 7 8 1 4 2 1 8 0 1 4 3 8 *